813

WANTON MALLY

*"The Versailles smile that expressed a gentleman's
detachment from whatever happened to him."*

FROM THE PORTRAIT OF M. DE CHAMPVALLON BY LARGILLIÈRE

WANTON MALLY

By
Booth Tarkington

With drawings by
JOSEPH SIMONT

DOUBLEDAY, DORAN & COMPANY, INC.
GARDEN CITY   1932   NEW YORK

PRINTED AT THE *Country Life Press*, GARDEN CITY, N. Y., U. S. A.

PS 3539
.A68 W3
1932

To

ELIZABETH STANLEY TROTTER
of Cleeve Gate

ILLUSTRATIONS

*"Two men and a woman on a black horse, a white horse and a bay horse—
all with blackened faces and wearing black cloaks."*

ILLUSTRATIONS

WANTON MALLY

*"Two men and a woman on a black horse, a white horse and a bay horse—
all with blackened faces and wearing black cloaks."*

CHAPTER I

ONSIEUR DE GRAMMONT, most light-hearted of all Seventeenth Century young gentlemen, and more light-hearted than ever in exile, was delighted one March morning, after too merry a night with King Charles at Whitehall, to receive a compatriot who was, like himself, youthful, a fine flower from the garden of Versailles, and bore gayly another resemblance even more striking. Like M. de Grammont, the caller had the honor of banishment at the hands of Louis XIV personally, so to say; moreover, the distinction had been conferred upon him only

some three-score hours earlier, and this Chevalier
de Champvallon stepped softly into M. de Grammont's bedchamber, spurred, cloaked and elabo-
rately stained with fast travel. There had been
rain in the north of France, and there were in-
numerable small poultices of dried mud upon his
boots, spurs and thin scabbard, upon his exquisite gauntlets embroidered with gold thread and
upon his beautiful blue cuirass; but the English
roads were dry and had powdered him impar-
tially everywhere. M. de Champvallon, though
instantly recognizable as a great fellow for good
lace and daintiness in dress, seemed unaware of
carrying the tokens of two national soils. Neither
fatigue nor this palpable evidence of flight from
one country to another seemed to trouble him;
apparently nothing troubled him or could be
permitted to alter the lift of his fine eyebrows
and the delicate extension of his lips in the Versailles smile that expressed a gentleman's proper
detachment from whatever either agreeably or
disagreeably happened to him.

M. de Grammont was being dressed while fin-
ishing his morning cup of chocolate; but he rose

to offer a formal embrace not devoid of real cordiality. "My dear friend! What surprise!"

"One to me also," M. de Champvallon said, as they sat and M. de Grammont's dressing continued. "But you are the last man to whom I need explain that a condition of astonishment is precisely the condition upon which one is admitted to be near the person of the Sun King. I am your comrade in two things: surprise and exile." M. de Champvallon, not rising, bowed appreciatively. "I am sensible of the honor."

"No; it is mine," M. de Grammont said, and bowed as gracefully. "I permit myself to imagine that you yourself may have surprised somebody and—"

"No; I am not so intrusive," M. de Champvallon interrupted, and increased his smile delicately. "The intrusion was upon myself, most unexpectedly, though it is true that I was at once charged with intrusion and by an august personage. But I accept the responsibility for demolishing my career: I knew perfectly that it is a crime to whisper in sea-shell ears behind the curtains of a window embrasure at Marly—that is, when those ears are precious to the august. My only excuse is that I did not know the grand old he-cat was so near."

"He-cat, my dear Champvallon?"

"Pardon my irreverence, my dear friend; I am so newly a fugitive. To me the Grand Monarch appears to have a touch of he-cattery. I beg you to recall that passage in Herodotus in which he describes those gentlemen, the he-cats of Egypt. You are not the only victim of a royal cannibalism no doubt imitated from the behavior of those gentlemen. Once more I have the honor to be your confrère."

"What happiness for me!" The two bowed again; M. de Grammont laughed, then looked at a shoe a valet was offering for inspection and gently waved it away. "No, not scarlet heels this morning," he said, and explained to de Champvallon, "The English are eager to improve themselves; they imitate me with such enthusiasm that within a few days after I have set a fashion I must again become original in order to avoid dressing like everybody. Herodotus, you said. I must remember to speak of that passage to the

King of England this evening. He will be delighted to hear that you made so happy a comparison between his cousin and the old he-cats of Egypt who slew all the young ones in order to prevent a subsequent rivalry."

M. de Champvallon sighed lightly. "I suppose it is a slander," he said, with a little compunction. "Perhaps we young he-cats are too given to thinking that someone is jealous of us, and also, it is difficult for us to know which of two things in a prince growing elderly we have offended. We like to think it is his jealousy; but it may be his sense of propriety. There is a great deal more propriety at Versailles since you left there, my dear friend. I will not flatter you; your absence has nothing to do with it. It is all because the Grand Monarch feels that at his age propriety captivates not only the celestial powers but his children's governess also."

"The little Scarron! My dear Champvallon, in your case, who was the lady?"

"The lady?" M. de Champvallon smiled reproachfully. "There were two, a circumstance proving that my life is shattered for mere pastime. But I hasten to assure you that neither of the ladies was Madame Scarron nor the one to whom your own pleasant whisperings brought a disturbance of the heart so perceptible as to over-heat the temper of Majesty. My two were less disturbed than was your one, and, as I am so much smaller a personage than yourself, the royal disturbance was not comparable to that you caused; but it was sufficient! I had a hurried choice between flight and Pignerol; I feared Pignerol might be mouldy. I reached the barbarous English coast at Dover last night in a fishing-boat, and here I am, asking advice of your experience."

"My dear friend!" M. de Grammont exclaimed benevolently. "I have better than experience to offer you."

"No, no! I am not here to plunder you of anything but wisdom; I have even a diamond or two to give away if need be. In truth I desire nothing but to ask you about these English. What species of animal are they?"

In spite of his benevolence M. de Grammont was a little relieved. "You have come to the right man, my dear Champvallon. My advice to you is to pass the time of exile in studying the customs and habits of the English; thus you will improve your mind and find entertainment. It is simple, for at this court you will not even need to know the language."

"But I do—perhaps even better than a Frenchman should. I suppose it is pardonable for a fugitive to praise himself like that. I accept your advice with gratitude and I begin my study of the English this very moment by learning all I can from you. How does one amuse oneself among them?"

M. de Grammont laughed inaudibly. "You will have no difficulty there, since they are all bent upon amusing themselves. A few years ago they were all devoutly forcing themselves into heaven by means of a piety based upon sermons and decapitations. Now they do nothing but what is outrageously in the comic spirit. You see, they lack our French stability of character; they are the most volatile people in the world, the English. They have not known how to do what we do in our settled state of society; they

do not from generation to generation go on living in the same way, with so much time given to
the church, so much to government, so much to
war, so much to gallantry, so much to the hu-
manities and the arts, so much to a cultivation of
the society of other beings as civilized as ourselves, and so much to acquiring a perfect comprehension of what food, wine and tailors should
be. In fact, they are not very civilized. They are
a people always in ferment, never poised in the
centre of things but always living in one barbarous extreme or the other. In a word, dear Champvallon, this is an epoch when they wish to make
the devil drunk and will get drunk with him.
You may do anything you please in England;
you may steal the Crown Jewels if your manner
of taking them makes the King laugh. Yet he is
a man not without some elegance—a great part
of his youth was spent in France. I will take you
to him this evening."

M. de Champvallon inclined his head in gratitude but smiled with a faint ruefulness. "That
is like your kindness, my friend; I will not press
upon it so heavily. No, I have heard it said that

when an Arab visits a hospitable stranger's tent
he should not bring his camel in with him—I
must not be your camel. I have a thought, too,
that the Sun King might not be so indulgent
with his English cousin in regard to me as he is
in your own affair. Letters might pass between
the King Louis and the King Charles, and a mere
little de Champvallon of the cadet branch might
be returned in the direction of Pignerol. Finally,
for myself, I have a small surfeit of association
with a king and a court."

"But what do you wish to do? These people
have nothing like the life of our châteaux; but
they do possess some heavy houses in the country, and if your fancies incline to the pas-
toral—"

"No," de Champvallon said, and lifted a protesting, slim hand. "My desires are all urban. I
should like to study the amusements of this London. Life in the country has no charm for me.
I confess you have said something that fasci-
nates me; you have declared that these people
have a trace of savagery in their merriment, and
I know enough of history to be sure that when

a people go to extremes their supreme extremity is always reached in their greatest town. My tastes are a little mad. If you will be so generous, direct me to the wild life of London."

"Willingly." M. de Grammont touched his forehead with a finger or two. "But you puzzle me, for what you seek is at court, and you say you will not go there. But wait! I will think." He plunged himself into some moments of cogitation; then brightened suddenly. "But yes! I have what you desire. Perfectly! Meestress Jeeny Feelmotte!"

"How?" de Champvallon asked, and for the moment had no comprehension that his friend had attempted to pronounce an English name. "What is that?"

"Meestress Jeeny Feelmotte," M. de Grammont replied decisively. "She is the right one for you. She is what you seek and she will also show you what you seek."

"You are speaking of somebody? Of a woman?"

"Of a woman decidedly."

M. de Champvallon's expression, remotely

amiable by habit, increased in affability. "Married? Beautiful?"

"Hélas! Neither," M. de Grammont said, and again laughed soundlessly. "Well, I must prepare you for her a little. She is like nothing that anything in your whole life in France could have led you to expect to see. For you, just arrived on this soil, many things in England are unimaginable; she most of all. Yet I must attempt a little portrait of her for you. I think one reason she is not married is that the only husband she could consider would be Master Satan, and she knows him well but finds him too decorous. You begin to catch a glimpse of her, my friend?"

"I begin to be profoundly interested. Continue, I beg."

"Very well. A moment of history will not fatigue you. You see, the revolution of those Fanatiques, some years ago, made all of England very gloomy, very dull; everything was Olivier Cronvell and sanctimony. Whatever was natural, gay or pretty was a sin. Now all that is overthrown, and in particular a new kind of woman has emerged. To comprehend her, you must not

think of the Mancini or of Mademoiselle de
Lenclos. They are only examples of something
that is always produced at intervals by any civili-
zation; the new woman of England is the rep-
resentative of this new epoch; Mademoiselle
Feelmotte is the apex of a revolution against the
old revolution; she is the extreme of a class of
young people who hate with venom everything
that is old-fashioned, hypocritical and restrict-
ing. They abolish everything except frankness
and liberty. Mademoiselle Feelmotte believes a
woman may do anything that a man may, and
she does! I should add that she has followers of
both sexes who sometimes finds themselves stag-
gering in the effort to keep pace with her. You,
my dear Champvallon, will be equal to her and
yet remain upon your feet. I speak in admiration born of some knowledge of you."

"I thank you," M. de Champvallon said, responding with gravity to a twinkle in his friend's
eye. "You insist that she has no beauty?"

"Oh, I do not go so far! Her face is thought
an odd one—delicately moulded but not by the
best of sculptors, and perhaps a little yellow. She

does not permit this to discourage her, for she
possesses and uses most adroitly those compen-
sations with which Madame Venus seeks to console ladies whose faces are not called pretty. Extraordinary eyes, extraordinary hair. The eyes
lovely, not to be read and perhaps a little sly;
the hair a blonde marvel, superbly curled. The
form as magnificent as the eyes and hair and as
freely made known to you; the voice low, a little
husky and as ready to say anything as she is to
do anything. For a final stroke upon my canvas,
she is not so rich as our own Grande Montpen-
sier; but she is rich. She is an orphan, keeps her
guardians in a swoon and last month set fire to
a tavern because the food displeased her."

"You have done the same thing to me!" M. de
Champvallon exclaimed, with a pleasant anima-
tion. "Not I hope because I displease you! I am
overcome by your kindness and also by the pene-
tration that perceives so precisely what I had
hoped to find in London. When may I be led into
the presence of this enchanting wickedness?"

"Éh, not so fast! I will not give you up so
quickly," M. de Grammont said. "Once you are

with her I shall not soon see you again. In the afternoon I will deliver you to each other. Now we shall have breakfast, and then I think you should have an hour or two of repose before—"

"Repose!" The more recent of the two exiles looked at the other aggrievedly. "Repose for me, my friend?"

"Ah, pardon, pardon!" de Grammont cried, as his servants placed a table between himself and his guest. "My memory is as infamous as your sleeplessness is famous. I recall that it was spiteful little St. Simon who said, 'Champvallon never rests; he should be a sentry'. Again this Meestress Jeeny Feelmotte is the right one for you! One morning when the King of England awoke he asked for the news and someone told him it was said in the town that Mademoiselle Feelmotte had slept peacefully for several hours the previous night. The King said he had asked for news not for lies, and I prefer not to tell you what else he said. I have talked enough; now tell me all the news of Versailles—and then in two or three hours I will surrender you to your study of this new woman and her barbarians."

M. de Champvallon's modesty urged him to look doubtful for a moment, and he yielded to the pressure, inclining his head a little toward one shoulder. "But of course we have not ascertained that this demoiselle will be willing to undertake my education. It is only too well known how often I have failed in my efforts to please the most honest ladies."

"Ah, traitor!" M. de Grammont cried, and wagged a chiding, white forefinger at him. "I am like the King of England; I have asked for news and not for lies. Mademoiselle Feelmotte will throw herself at my feet in gratitude for you!"

CHAPTER II

M. DE GRAMMONT employed a figure of speech well warranted by the event. The famous Mrs. Jinny Wilmot did not indeed prostrate her fine person before him; but she was as grateful as if she had made that gesture. Somewhat dulled in enthusiasm for the riot she called pleasure, in the Chevalier de Champvallon she perceived something new—at least a new stimulant to continue the riot. Here was a new companion rioter for her and also a new audience she could hope to astonish, though that proved a little difficult. M. de Champvallon's

17

disposition was of an incomparable sang-froid, one that almost dazzled her; she determined to shatter his calm at all costs. He declined to be surprised by anything, and she was accustomed to surprise everybody; this was her great vanity and she lived for it. Within a week she was furious because of his continued calm; she suspected that she had fallen in love with him and felt that her suffering might become intolerable if she did not succeed in astonishing him.

The field of her operations in her assault upon the Chevalier de Champvallon's placidity was a city blithe to show the sign of a mad world—a London wherein sober gentlemen, for some were often sober, might tremble to be out alone at night; a rowdy London unlighted, of breakneck, dirty streets where dangerously ranged, all "flown with insolence and wine", such cockerel bands as the Tityre Tus and Harry Killigrew's Ballers; a drunken London that saw baronets strip themselves in public and run howling to fight with the Watch; a masterless London where thieves sang in their own coffee-houses and robbers fought duels over the spoils of easy violence;

a licentious London where in daytime roisterers seized upon masked women in the streets and willy-nilly made them caper. Nay, it was the London where the mighty heretic-baiter, Bishop Bourne, hero of lawful citizens for his hatred of the Quakers, was struck down at last twilight in his chair as he came to his own very door from a vesper sermon he had preached against that perilsome sect. The profanation was done by three mounted rogues with blackened faces, and, what seemed most horrid to the Bishop's defenders, one of the three was discerned to be a woman, riding like a man.

The Bishop was shot through his upper body by one of his own frightened servants, no great marksman; but the confusion was lively, the dusk misty and the rogues rode straight against the chair, setting up a rackety flailing of it with swords and a shrill shouting of "Your purse or your life, rascal Bishop!" No one except the poor marksman himself knew who had exploded a pistol, and he did not tell. Instead, he ran to fiery Colonel Bourne, the Bishop's brother, with the dreadful news that the robbers had done this sacrilegious murder, and the Colonel was not long in being after them with a squad of horse. The two highwaymen and the highwaywoman had the Bishop's purse just as he was shot, and they rode off, laughing like three jackanapeses.

But here at last was a thing that stirred some sense of legality in London, and even in King Charles. He took an oath to hang those three, and, whether the Bishop lived or died, there was wrath not only in the town but over half of England.

A London where such things might be was precisely the spot to M. de Champvallon's taste, more than ever since he was a student of it under the tutelage of the lady M. de Grammont had recommended to him. On that account, it at first appears to be strange that upon a foggy morning, not a month after his call upon his fellow exile, he should have found himself riding thoughtfully a tired horse in a wilderness of moorland a long way from London. Moreover, to say that he found himself is to hint less than the truth; himself was all that he could find. It is true he had at times a suspicion that he was near the sea—or, at least, one of the seas that gird the great island—for there came fitfully to his ears a sound like that of heavy waters boisterous among rocks, and once or twice, overhead, he thought he heard a plaintive conversation of sea-fowl that flew invisibly through the fog.

True, too, he knew the name of the moor, for Mrs. Jinny Wilmot had told him it was called Wanton Mally, when at dawn she had set him on the almost imperceptible path by which he was meant to cross it. But one may know that he is on a planet called by some the Earth, and yet have no knowledge of what position he occupies in space; thus the Chevalier knew he was in the midst of something called Wanton Mally, yet was unaware of its location and so found the name itself of slight avail. Under other circumstances—that is to say, if he had not been again a fugitive with a king urging the pursuit of him —he might have been interested in this name of Wanton Mally. For it was an ancient one suitable to a student's investigation and a point at issue among the learned in philology, inciting quarrels in their debates upon it. There was a

half-lost road across the moor; this zig-zag semblance was also named Wanton Mally and called
"the Mally", supplying added confusion to both
the traveller and the debater, for the so-called
road, as well as its name, bore faint suggestions
of a debauched and conscienceless sort of mall.
Only flatterers could have accepted such suggestions for the truth, or fallen in with the local
habit of speaking of two other vague tracks
across the waste as paths; and it was one of these
that M. de Champvallon had wholly lost within
ten minutes after Mrs. Jinny, still sooty about
the eyes in spite of a brookside washing, had set
him upon it.

Proud to be philosophic, he lacked the habit of
blaming and only wondered that he had not lost
himself sooner. It was no fault of his indeed that
he was lost; the moor could easily have done that
to him without the fog. Wanton Mally was an
unending wasteland of fen, strewn rock, stag-
gered ravine and dismal copse; and if the Chevalier had known that badgers inhabited
certain parts of it, as they did, he would have
pitied them. The last village he had seen in his

flight from London with Mrs. Jinny and her
fellow-harebrain, Rafe Chedlowe, was Littlefield, and there, after resisting a desperate temp-
tation to eat and rest at a tavern, the three had
the belated wisdom to separate and take the three
different ways across Wanton Mally. For these
three ways, the two paths and the road of Wanton Mally, entered the moor almost together near
Littlefield; then diverged and met again five
miles from Mally Surfeit, which stands beyond
the farther border of the waste.

This Mally Surfeit, beyond the moor, was no
more than a sparse hamlet of stone and thatch
about a little church and a big brick barn of a
manor house where dwelt Mr. Brunnage, the
great man of those parts. This is not to say that
Mr. Brunnage was a great man; but where there
is nothing a little something seems great, and Mr.
Brunnage was a little something. Not to under-
rate him, he was even a magistrate; he believed
in the Church of England, the kingship, mutton
and the iron hand upon all poachers, non-con-
formists, papists and vagrants.

When he would be comfortable at home he re-

laxed from his spurred heavy boots and his flow-
ing curled periwig, which was subject to nits;
but when he rode forth to any distance he had
boots, spurs, periwig and no doubt some nits
upon him, and added an old Cavalier's corselet
to his other gear. Thus, riding in the fog, this
same morning, while M. de Champvallon wandered upon the moor, he clinked dauntingly
when button or buckle touched his front, or
scabbard swung against stirrup or spur; there
were pistols in his holsters, and he smelt of old
metal, of damp old cloth, of greased leather and
strong ale. Behind him rode two heavy minions
of his from the stone and thatch village, themselves mostly stone and thatch but armed like
their master and smelling much like him, though
not so much, for now it was past March, and, as
the first of April had been a day hot beyond its
season, they had swum in the tide-water that
reaches by Mally Surfeit.

Mr. Brunnage and his two fellows rode slowly
but not because they were doubtful of the way;
they knew the moor in any fog and their dull
gait was to help them listen. They had come to a

low hillock straddled by this road of Wanton
Mally, when the leader drew rein and the three
sat their saddles in silence to hear the more
keenly. They could see little except themselves,
their steeds and the rough ground close about
them; but somewhere, off to the left, all three
heard a horse shake himself and then a delicate
and peculiarly reserved coughing, a man's. Mr.
Brunnage turned in his saddle and made two gestures, whereupon his two servants rode quietly
to the left but separating as if they followed two
sides of a triangle, the apex of which was Mr.
Brunnage. He remained some moments, motionless; then, walking his horse, rode down the middle of this imagined triangle and had gone about
forty yards when he saw, straight before him,
movements of a faint pinkish color in the grey
vapor, hints of a tinted silhouette. Within the
moment he came face to face with a wan young
gentleman riding a muddy-legged bay horse and
dressed principally in wet rose velvet as if he had
come (through rain) from a gavotte at Whitehall. He did not even wear boots; his fawn shoes
had gilt heels.

"Stand, you!" Mr. Brunnage said roughly, and, at the sound of his voice, his two men emerged into visibility, turning in, one upon each of the stranger's flanks. "What's your name and purpose?"

M. de Champvallon removed his broad hat plumed with fawn-colored ostrich feathers that made a little shower with this motion. "My purpose?" he said in a faintly protesting voice, and with so slight a foreign accent that his boast to M. de Grammont was somewhat warranted. The Chevalier de Champvallon (M. de Grammont would have agreed) spoke English as well as a Frenchman need speak anything but French; nevertheless, the accent was perceptible. "My purpose? Firs' to salute you, sir, and nex' to ask you tell me in the name of 'eaven 'ow can one dispatch oneself out of this Vanton Mallee?"

"Body and bones!" Mr. Brunnage cried fiercely. "What's this? A Dutchman?"

"I do not seem to be," the young man answered. "But I 'ave no certainties remaining in my soul."

"I'll have certainties from you!" Mr. Brunnage promised him sternly. "I asked for your name. Speak out!"

"I still think I am the Chevalier de Champvallon."

"Shove-along! Shove-along! What's that?"

"Me," M. de Champvallon returned mildly. "I think it is the way you speak my name."

"Looky!" the frowning Brunnage said, and shook a forefinger at the young Frenchman. "I be out to catch rogues; I'll not dally with you. Who are you, what are you and wha' d' you do here? I have a stone cell at Mally Surfeit for them as won't answer such questions!"

"But I do answer," M. de Champvallon said politely. "Willingly! I 'ave tell you I am the Chevalier de Champvallon and what I do now is to drip all over this Vanton Mallee because I wish to be somewhere else and cannot because it seem' there is nothing else anywhere. I think to myself, 'Surely there is somewhere else but this Vanton Mallee lef' in the worl'!' Sir, will you tell me 'ow I can discover it?"

"I'll tell you how you can discover my cell at Mally Surfeit if you don't—"

"A moment!" the young man said urbanely. "I comprehend. You are per'aps an officer in charge of the good be'avior of people who lose themself in this—"

"I'll prove to you who I be," Mr. Brunnage said, "if you do not—"

"But I do! Sir, do you know Monsieur de Grammont?"

"Musseer de Grammont?" Mr. Brunnage, surprised by this mention of King Charles's favored French intimate, modified his tone; yet still spoke gruffly. "What have you to do with Musseer de Grammont?"

"Ah, too much! If it was not for that great comedian, Monsieur de Grammont, I should not be in this Vanton Mallee."

"You tell me you be a friend of his?"

"Can one be a frien' of a man who will do a such thing to 'im? But yes, I am the mos' loyal in this worl'; I forgive 'im and remain 'is frien'. I will make myself plain to you. Since we begin to talk my 'ead grow more clear. Now I become certain I am not Dutch; I am French like Monsieur de Grammont and of the court of the King

of France. I was in London to see my frien',
Monsieur de Grammont, and 'e advise' me 'ow to
improve myself. I travel. I travel to study the
be'avior and custom' of your great English people. I did wish to go everywhere; but that was a
mistake because it mus' be true that this Vanton
Mallee is a part of everywhere, and for that reason I should not 'ave wish' to go everywhere. No
people live 'ere; the English are intelligent. I cannot study them where they are not; that is why
I ask you to 'elp me to find where they are."

"So!" Mr. Brunnage was contemptuous of all
this foreign fol-de-rol of speech; but he was less
severe. This Musseer Shove-along might indeed
be what he laid claim to be, a friend of the magnificent Musseer de Grammont who joked every
night with King Charles. By nature and long
habit, Mr. Brunnage was of a brow-beating bent,
truculent and given to smelling out rascalities
even where there were none; but it is wisdom to
make a friend of a friend of a friend of a king.
The lost young gentleman's dampened garb was
recognizably an exquisite courtier's;—to be sure,
it was grotesque for travel and mad upon Wan-

ton Mally. But he was foreign, so much so as to be a Frenchman, and where was ever a Frenchman who did anything that a creature with reason could explain? Moreover, Mr. Brunnage had not come forth to lay hold of a single horseman; he sought a group of three suspected of being far worse than French. He began to speak mildly. "Well, you may be what you say; if so, I'll deal no harder with you than set you on your way. But have you any means to prove it?"

M. de Champvallon drew off his embroidered left gauntlet and showed a white hand and an emerald seal-ring. "I am sure you 'ave knowledge of the device' borne by the noble 'ouses of other kingdoms as well as your own," he said. "You recognize this of de Champvallon?"

Mr. Brunnage looked at the ring; it was splendid, awed him a little and completed a persuasion that he dealt with a personage of peculiar eminence. He was satisfied and even deferential. "No need, no need," he said. "I know satin from sacking when I see it. I hadn't no real suspicion of you and was rough spoken only in duty, which

a man o' your parts would easy know how to
understand."

"Ah, a thousan' time'!" M. de Champvallon
said graciously, and brought forth an enamelled
gold boxlet of scented snuff. "May I offer you?"

"Thanky, thanky," the Squire said, availing
himself liberally of a rare opportunity. He
powdered his nose and upper lip, sniffing power-
fully; the Chevalier, with increasing gracious-
ness, partook delicately, and the completed cere-
mony seemed to tincture the thick air with a
mutual respect and something like goodfellow-
ship. "Noble stuff, sir!" Mr. Brunnage said.
"Though the truth is I ha'n't no fine coffee-
house manners and be more for my pipe than
this nose-tickling. Yet, oicks! I can nose-tickle,
too, if I be a-mind. Well, sir, getting on with
my duty, would you permit me to ask you a question for the law's information?"

"A question? A thousan'!"

"Well, then, have you fell in with three riders, two men and a woman, last night or to-day,
or have you seen such a three on the moor or out
of it?"

"Two men and a woman?" The young man seemed to search his memory. "Two men and a woman. No; in all this place I 'ave seen nobody. Not a soul."

"Did you come by Littlefield?"

"I cannot say. Is it a city? Stop! I know—it is where I should 'ave res' las' night and not come into this place."

"So! Then you've been on the moor all night. Well, you wouldn't have seen 'em unless it was this morning, for they were not at Littlefield until half an hour before full daylight. It may be the better for you that you had no sight of 'em, Musseer Shove-along."

"Éh? Some bad people?"

" 'Bad'!" Mr. Brunnage repeated, and his nostrils rose, expanding. "If it's hanging for 'em instead of the stake—the stake and slow burning —then I say England's daft! There's more in what they did than London knows. More behind it than plain sacrilegious murder and robbery. More behind it, sir, more behind it!"

"You say?" M. de Champvallon inquired, seeming to listen with patient interest; but his

foreign pronunciation became more evident.
"Somesing you say some bad people did do?"

"Looky!" Mr. Brunnage cried. "I'll take 'em!
I'll have 'em by nightfall, and what Brunnage
promises Brunnage does!"

M. de Champvallon bowed gravely and repeated the name with a little difficulty. "Bron-
age? That is you, sir?"

"Me, sir? Yes, sir!" Mr. Brunnage returned
with emphasis. "Brunnage. Keep that name in
your memory, Musseer Shove-along, and add to
it that I sit at Mally Surfeit as a Justice. Brunnage, Musseer Shove-along, Brunnage!" Mr.
Brunnage had his natural reasons for desiring the
friend of a king's favorite to remember the name,
and, for these same reasons, he became expan-
sive. "I'll tell you this thing, Musseer Shove-
along. Looky how 'twas. Night afore last, these
two he-rogues and their she-rogue murdered the
properest churchman in England, my lord Bishop
Bourne, hard by his own doorstep in London
town. Robbed and murdered him, sir! Col'nel
Bourne rode after 'em and was close; but there
was this same fog over all the country and it's

like they was cunning and lay hid in a wood through the daylight yesterday. He came into Littlefield betimes this morning and they had been there, because the tavern-keeper looked from a window, saw 'em stop and then go on. So Col'nel Bourne sends a fisherman to me in his boat, and the man rows up Wanton Water to find me at my house in Mally Surfeit and tell me what's afoot. Other men went out from Littlefield to rouse all the country behind the moor; but Bourne was sure the three fiends are on Wanton Mally. Two men and a woman on a black horse, a white horse and a bay horse, and keeping together—the woman on the white horse and riding shameless like a man—and all three with blackened faces and wearing black cloaks."

"Strange," M. de Champvallon said reflectively. "A strange appearance."

Mr. Brunnage laughed shrewdly. "But all the easier to be catched! Col'nel Bourne's beating 'em up from Littlefield; but I be the man that'll take 'em by candle-lighting for a thousand pound! They still had their faces blacked when they came into Littlefield, and good reason,

"Two men and a woman on a black horse, a white horse and a bay horse—all with blackened faces and wearing black cloaks."

too, that they would not be known where I
swear one o' the three *would* be known. I'll wash
that riddle off his face for him with my own
hands, Musseer Shove-along, and show a skin folk
here have hateful knowledge of! Bourne's fisherman did not tell me half when I began to smell
that skin and what else was behind this foulness.
Plotting, Musseer Shove-along, deep plotting and
murder done against church and king by the infidel."

"Who? You say the infidel?"

"Why, looky now! There's a roguey knave
been living on this very Wanton Mally these last
three year, one that's known to hate all laws and
observances of God and man, one that's for-
sworn church and king and joined himself to
desperate villains, male and female, of the same
mind that are a curse upon a hundred parts of
England and shall be stamped on! Now hark to
me, Musseer Shove-along; this fellow, Colpoys,
rode to London ten days ago and's not home, for
I rode straight from Mally Surfeit to his house,
and he's looked for there by candle-lighting this
night. What's it mean?"

"I cannot tell."

"Why, he was in London when the Bishop was murdered; there's men there and women, too, of his own kind that'd help him do it, and where would he come and bring them when he'd done it? Why, straight here as he could ride, to lie run to ground in his own earth. But I be the earth-stopper that'll stop him! What's more, I be the one man of substance and authority in England that can bear the right witness against him. Hark to me now: What was it the Bishop preached against within the hour of their horrid-ness?"

M. de Champvallon was wholly unaware. "I cannot tell you."

"Why, the very pestilents this fellow, Col-poys, has joined!" the Justice cried. "I've all points of the matter, sir; they make a case that damns him. He's a Quaker, the Bishop preached against Quakers, Colpoys was there, now he's riding here upon the spot where it's known the murderers ride. I'll find him with a he and she Quaker with him, and what more's needed?"

"Quecka," the French gentleman murmured,

finding the word not of his vocabulary. "It mean' a wicked fellow?"

"Vipers beyond thinking!" Mr. Brunnage assured him, with passion. "What's those who hate the law and the church, set themselves to destroy both, swear openly they despise the King, and murder bishops?"

"That poor Bishopp," M. de Champvallon said, and seemed to become reflective. "Éh, but it is a great misfortune!"

"One that'll be suffered for, sir; rest your soul on that!"

"I belief," the young man said, "I should be upon my way. If you will show me—"

"Be easy; I'll not keep you." Mr. Brunnage gave him a narrow glance and went to the point of the conversation. "They say all goes by favor at court, and great service to the crown has little reward unless there's some there to press for it. When I take these rogues it may be Col'nel Bourne or another as'll get praise and more for it unless the truth find means to reach the King. Now I'll put you on your way so that you'll not lose it, whereby you may think I do you a small service, Musseer Shove-along."

"Ah, a great one—to save me from this desolation—"

"Well, since you take it as a kindness from me, I'll thanky to remember the name o' Brunnage when next you see your friend Musseer de Grammont. He could mention it to the King without trouble to himself—a word of what I've been telling you, how it's me that'll both catch and convict these profaners and murderers, a hint of my diligence and duty in this matter, if you take me? Maybe a word, too, of how I succored Musseer de Grammont's friend out of a distress—"

"A word? A thousan' in your praise will be too little, Misterr Bron-age. But if you please—"

"Never fear! What town had you a mind to come at this night?"

"Town? I do not care. My desire is for an inn with a fire and a dish one can eat. I do not care where it is; I only wish to arrive to it."

"No hard matter," Mr. Brunnage said, set his horse in motion, turned him about, and, within the minute, showed M. de Champvallon the road of Wanton Mally. "There. There's the Mally. You can follow that well enough. It'll take you out o' the moor and at its end you'll find yourself upon a King's Highway not to be mistook. Ride thither a little briskly and you'll not be stopped. I had three fellows with me earlier; but, when I found Colpoys abroad, I went beyond his house, then sent one back to bring men from Mally Surfeit to watch the joining of the road and the Highway. By noon they'll be there and all the edges of the moor'll be watched by them of Mally Surfeit, Littlefield and other parts; but, going easily, you'll be on the Highway in good time and go unquestioned. Do you turn right on the Highway and go seven mile to the Stag's Horn at Kennelton, lie there to-night and you'll not be sorry. They'll put you on the road for London in the morning and I'll trust you not to forget the service Brunnage did you, when you see your friend."

"Never! I shall tell 'im—"

"Well," Mr. Brunnage said, "I'll say farewell to you, though you may see me again. It might be I'd come up with you on this very road and

bring three trussed fiends in my charge." He
turned with his men to move farther down the
Mally; but, at a thought, drew rein. "Ah, there's
another thing you might remember to speak a
word on o' Brunnage—how you saw me ride off
with only two at my back to catch 'em, and they
known to be very desperate rogues."

"I will tell 'im," M. de Champvallon said
gravely. "I promise Monsieur de Grammont shall
'ave the pleasure to 'ear everysing that 'as pass'
between you and me, Misterr Bron-age."

CHAPTER III

M R. BRUNNAGE had said comfortably
that the young Frenchman could
follow the road of Wanton Mally well enough,
and it is true that he did follow it, though at the
cost of dismounting some score of times to look
for it. He seemed also to search for something
else a little higher in the fog; but when at last he
found it his nose not his eyes most availed him.
Through the vapors about him there stole an
aromatic suggestion; he sniffed and was sure of a
smell of wood-smoke. He rode onward, then
smelled nothing; turned back and caught the

hint of smoke again. Putting faith in his nose, he risked leaving the feeble track of road and bore to his left, recalling emphatic instruction received from Mrs. Jinny Wilmot, for it was hers he followed now and not Mr. Brunnage's. M. le Chevalier de Champvallon, indeed, was seeking neither the Stag's Horn inn nor the King's Highway of which the Justice had told him, and, in spite of all that fol-de-rol of protestation he had made, he was not even striving to be free of Wanton Mally.

A minute or two of careful smoke-smelling brought him what he desired, a long silhouette of deeper grey that became, as he approached it, a long house, low, with lower dependent wings and all of old stone and sagging thatch. From a wide doorway of the wing nearer him a brown cow looked forth absently, as if committed to a revery in which a cavalier in rose velvet had no place; outside the opening, an old blue cart seemed to brood upon its abandonment, and beyond this wing were stables, sheds and vacant sheepfolds. M. de Champvallon passed by the cow, making as little of her as she of him; he applied himself to a door in the middle part of the house, for there he saw the windows were ruddy, and, dismounting, knocked politely. That is to say, he knocked politely for a time but later became more practical and this had the right effect.

A man in faded green cloth and worn leather opened the door and stared with expressionless grey eyes set in a brown face under thickets of weather-bleached tow hair. "Well?" he said, and the young man before him thought the cow as expressive. "Well?"

"It is the 'ouse of Misterr Colpoys?"

"He's abroad."

"So I 'ave been tol'," M. de Champvallon said, and added, with a thoughtful eye upon the man's face, "Misterr Bron-age did tell me. You know 'im?"

The reply was indifferent. "Ay, Squire was by."

"Tell me," the young Frenchman said, and turned to point in the direction whence he had come. "Yonder, not far, is the road of Vanton

Mallee. Somewhere near are two paths that come to it and all three meet?"

"Ay, they do."

"And this is the 'ouse of Misterr Colpoys, so I 'ave done well, but by a miracle! Tell me now, who is 'ere in this 'ouse?"

"None but me."

"Nobody?"

"None but me."

"Well, I will come in," M. de Champvallon said, and proffered the reins by which, with no necessity, he held his drooping steed. "Take this poor 'orse to the stable."

"The Master's afar," the man returned, not moving. "I look for him scarce afore nightfall."

"What?" M. de Champvallon said, and his eyes opened as if he were slightly startled. "You did not 'ear me? Take my 'orse, rub 'im well, give 'im water and in an hour some bran mix' with a little warm wine. You can 'ear me now?"

M. de Champvallon had not spoken with emphasis or in a higher key than usual; but apparently the stolid servitor thought best to pay heed. He took the reins, led the horse away, and

M. de Champvallon, entering the house, went
straight to sit upon a settle by the fire and
warm himself. The room, a kind of middle hall,
was big, low-ceiled and poor; M. de Champvallon saw nothing in it except the two settles by
the fireplace, a rough table and a few cumbersome oaken chairs—furniture that made him sigh
and oddly shake his head. A strange creature, this
Colpoys, plainly. How could a man once the
familiar of Mlle Jeeny Feelmotte bring himself
to live so meagerly and in such a house—worse,
in a house grovelling upon Vanton Mallee, this
eternity of a desert obviously created by that
chef des demons, Monsieur Satan!

But M. de Champvallon warm was M. de
Champvallon hungry; he called, "Hé! Hé!" and
clapped his hands loudly yet found himself still
alone. He went to the door where he had entered,
shouted from there without result, tried another
door and was in a bedroom that had nothing but
a bed in it. He passed into a dim, big kitchen and
here he opened a window, shouted again and was
answered by other shouting; but this came, it
seemed, from the hall where he had warmed him-

self. Thither he returned, therefore, to find the
hall empty though noisy with a thumping upon
the outer door.

"A little patience," he said, and opened the
door.

Outside there stood, as he himself had stood
half an hour earlier, a damp young man and a
gloomy horse equally damp. The horse was black
and so was the young man's periwig; but other-
wise the human being displayed gay brocades,
satin and lace, all flaccid with the wet. He was
tall, stoutly made, comely in a dark way and had
the true harebrain's eye, sparkling but not sane.

"Champvallon!" he cried. "Is Jinny safe? She's
here?"

The Chevalier shook his head. "My poor Chedlowe, nobody is 'ere. Nobody but me."

"But this is Colpoys's house?"

"Yes, but empty of 'im."

Mr. Chedlowe's bright, odd eyes showed quick
anger. "You're of an easy mind then, with Jinny
lost or catched somewhere behind us?"

"No; I am obedient. She tell us to come 'ere
and wait till we three will be join' again."

"You say you've not seen—"

"Nothing. Nothing but a piece of rock I think is the servant of Misterr Colpoys."

"Then I'll go back for her!"

"No," M. de Champvallon said serenely. "She will come. You 'ave arrive' 'ere; I 'ave arrive' 'ere, and neither you nor I know 'ow to do it. She does know. I will shout again for that piece of rock, and you will come in."

But now, surprisingly, the stony servant, coming from within the house, stepped by M. de Champvallon in the doorway and was recognized by Mr. Chedlowe, who called him by name. "Éh, Lecky? Still with Mr. Colpoys? He's abroad, this gentleman tells me; but I'll wait for him. Look to my horse."

"And in the name of the good Saint Bernard," M. de Champvallon cried, as Lecky with some readiness took the reins from Mr. Chedlowe's hand, "look to some food also for two gentlemen who will eat the straw roof of this 'ouse if you are not quick to save it! I tell you," he added, when Chedlowe had come in and gone to the fireplace, "I do not think that this Colpoys would keep a good kitchen; but I 'ave seen a cow of 'is, and if they do nothing to supply us with some food I will make the attemp' myself to cook 'er."

"You're in spirits, are you?" Mr. Chedlowe returned, looking at him gloomily. "You think you do well for Jinny's sake, do you, to be here yourself?"

His high and nervous voice sounded overtones of a threatening testiness not agreeable to the young Frenchman, whose smile shaded toward gravity. There was no amiability between these two; the rather they had the air, in spite of M. de Champvallon's suavities, of mistrustful antagonists. Comrades, newly and temporarily, through great pressure, each had a hawkish eye for the other; but the manners of Mr. Chedlowe were the more brittle. "You think of her safety, do you?" he went on. "You know as I do it's three together they follow. So when she comes, here's the three of us again, with a bay horse, a black horse and a white horse in the stables!"

"My poor Chedlowe! I do not think the pursuit is very near; I 'ave some cause to belief those

who are the neares' are going the other way—
for a while. But it seem' to me I 'ave some reason
to ask the question: If a gentleman think it is
peril for a lady to be with 'im and another gentleman, then why does 'e not go to another
place? Me, I 'ave the opinion that by midday
there will be trouble for who might wish to de-
part from Vanton Mallee. I think you will still
'ave the time perhaps if you would make a little
'aste. You permit the suggestion?"

Mr. Chedlowe, standing with the fire close behind him, showed a face that seemed as well
warmed as his back. "I'll not have more words
with you, Champvallon! Yesterday in the copse
when we'd heard Col'nel Bourne speaking hard
by to his troopers I warned you 'twas your plain
duty to be off. Jinny knew I spoke soundly;
'twas her wish as well as mine, if you'd had eyes
to see it."

"Strange! Strange she did not say so."

"In her heart she wished it, Champvallon!"

" 'Er 'eart, my poor Chedlowe? Pardon, but
I think you do not know it; you are too ready to
speak its desire."

"I'm ready to speak upon some other matters, too!" Mr. Chedlowe returned with vigor. "I make no doubt you think Grammont could syrup the King for you if Col'nel Bourne come up with us and we're laid by the heels. You take it all so easy I see you think you're safe, and for aught I know it's your belief we all three could keep whole skins. I tell you fairly we made an ill venture of it with Jinny's 'Master-jest' to rob a bishop! It was the worst black fortune that ever befell a little tricky roistering. D'you think we'd ever find means to show we had no pistol amongst us, or who it was fired one, a thing we don't know, ourselves? Worse for us, 'twould be no matter if we could bring such evidence—no, nor more to show that what we did was for our sport! What we did was a hanging felony, no matter our intent or the result, and it's fifty times a hanging one since the Bishop had his hurt of it. I tell you if we're catched not Grammont nor the King himself if he had the mind could hold back the hangman from us, and I give you to know, Champvallon, the King'll have no such mind!"

"My poor Chedlowe! You cause yourself too great trouble to tell me what I know very well."

"Do you so? Do you so?" Chedlowe cried, and struck his right fist into his left palm in a gesture of petulant desperation. "Plague on it! You would keep with us and now there's no shedding you! The worst folly we did was to hold together! What easier for Bourne to follow than a bay horse, a white horse and a black horse, the white rode by a woman? And to put madness on folly we must needs keep the soot on our faces and ride in our black cloaks even until we'd passed through Littlefield this very morning's dawn. If we forgot to do one thing to get us catched I have no news of it!"

M. de Champvallon, leaning negligently upon the back of one of the settles, regarded him with a whimsical commiseration. "My poor Chedlowe, I fear you do not remember that all these artifice' were devise' by the daughter of glory. She 'as a wit always quick in both attack and retreat. Let me show you 'er wisdom. She paint' Colonel Bourne a picture to set in 'is thought. She make it so plain to 'im 'e can think of nothing else.

Hour upon hour, two night' and a day, 'e follow that same picture, w'ich is three 'orses together—always together, a black 'orse, a white 'orse and a bay 'orse—and on these 'orses a woman and two men with black face' and black cloak'. She give 'im this picture all the way to Vanton Mallee, so it is expressly that picture 'e is certain 'e mus' catch in this Vanton Mallee. Then, pouf! she destroy' that picture; it no longer exis'! She say, 'Now, quick we wash our face' in the brook, 'ide our black cloak' under some rock' in the bottom of that brook; then we go by three different way'.' That big Bourne 'e look for 'is picture—well, we are not part of it and there is nothing for 'im to catch. 'E follow a thing that is disappear' in the fog. Our Jeeny, she 'as the brain of Henri le Grand, and I will tell her so when she arrive' to make 'erself dry, to eat and take res'."

"Rest? We're to take our rest?" the Englishman asked bitterly. "With Col'nel Bourne coming up, belike, to find those horses in Colpoys's stables and ourselves in the house!"

M. de Champvallon looked thoughtful. "Éh,

this Colpoys," he said, with curiosity. "What of 'im? Our Jeeny command us to meet at 'is 'ouse and I think she know' very easily the way to it, herself. Yet she say to me she did not see 'im for a long time. Once she know 'im very well, you think?"

"Know him well?" Mr. Chedlowe said, and his gloomy brow was quickly gloomier. "Better than she knows you, Monsieur Champvallon. When we ran for it, headed straight for Wanton Mally, didn't she? Not the first time she's been here, Monsieur Champvallon, nor the second, neither."

"So? You know this Colpoys, I think?"

"Tom Colpoys? If Jinny and me had took into our heads to frolic with a bishop three years ago, he'd have been the other man with us, not you, Champvallon. As hard a drinking, gaming, duelling, watch-baiting lover of all women as the town ever suffered to strut—a powerful-bodied man full of prankish conceits, and fought Sir Charles Sudeley with a knotted rope against a pike and left him tied in thorn-hedge. Jinny Wilmot was come to make a noise in the town then, too, and made most of it at him. I'll say

no more o' that, and care to know no more of it,
myself; but three years ago, after a time when
they were most together and seen everywhere at
their sports, he was gone all at once."

"Gone? Where he go?"

Young Mr. Chedlowe gave utterance to a
grudging laugh. "That was a question asked in
more and wickeder places than the coffee-houses,
I can tell you!" he said, and seemed nothing loth
to continue the subject; for jealousy, like anything else, will run in ancient grooves so that
those in its grip make always the same recurrent
clatter. Mr. Chedlowe talked willingly of Colpoys, and the Chevalier de Champvallon listened
with eagerness, because two men or two women,
jealous of each other and ready to be at swords'
points, must always call a truce and thus talk
and listen when there is mention of a third of
whom there may be jealousy. "With the town so
much the quieter for Colpoys not being in it,"
Mr. Chedlowe went on, "there could not help be
wonder where the noise was gone. Well, there
was no telling, and Jinny flew in a fury, for she
thought she ought to know, she of all the world,

and she did not. I think 'twas nigh a twelve-month passed 'fore ever she had wind of what he'd done, and came here and found him to have the matter out. Well, I can't say what happened between 'em then or other times she came here; I only know she did come here and stayed days in some kind of quarrelling with him, and every time came back to London in a greater fury than she went, and swore and said he'd mocked her. I know that much because she told it to Biddy Charigoe and Biddy told me. Jinny would never so much as speak his name to me, and we had hard words when I pressed her; so I tell you I had my own thoughts o' the matter this morning when she named his house for us to meet at. Now there's the riddle for you, Monsieur Champvallon; read it if you can."

M. de Champvallon's color had heightened, and, for the time, the last trace of his Versailles smile was gone. " 'Ow long you think since she saw 'im?" he asked.

"Biddy Charigoe told me last week 'twould be nearer a se'enmonth than one; but she hath sent letters to him—a score in that time, Biddy blabbed to me, with little answer from him to any of 'em. There's constancy for you—hers, I mean."

At this, M. de Champvallon again smiled. "Constancy? No, my poor Chedlowe. For one moment I was not able to read the riddle of our Jeeny and this Colpoys. Now I 'ave it! She would not let the man escape from 'er. At Fontaine-bleau the Marquis de Vesle 'ad forty-six little silver cups in 'is closet. Sometime' 'e would look at them but not often, for so long as 'e know they were there 'e care' nothing about them. Then one day 'e count them and one was missing; you would 'ave thought it 'is very life, 'e make' a such outcry! Some ladies are like that, and I will deal so fairly with you that I will tell you this secret about Jeeny, since it is what you say of Misterr Colpoys that make' it better known to me. To 'old 'er in one's 'and, one need' only to go away from 'er. There! Am I generous?"

But Mr. Chedlowe did not seem appreciative; the truce was at an end. "Generous, are you, Champvallon? You think you are so much advantaged with her you can toss me alms? Not

you! More, I let you know you're no riddle,
whether she be or not. If she'll follow who runs
from her, why don't you run, yourself? If she's
simple as that, you test it! I'll stay here and be
with her while you win her by going into hiding.
So there's a generosity to match yours, if you
take me."

"My poor Chedlowe! Let me tell you our
Jeeny—"

But upon this the Englishman was openly
truculent. "Enough o' your 'poor Chedlowes'
and 'our Jeenys'! First of all I'm not yours and
I'm not poor, and Jinny's not divided between
you and me. I'm not the man to brook such divi-
sions, even if they be the French custom, Champvallon!"

M. de Champvallon looked at him seriously
and was deliberate in replying. "Mr. Chedlowe, I
am waiting for a lady. I am not free until I 'ave
set 'er once more at 'er own 'ouse in safety. The
nex' moment after that is done, I shall ask you
please go with me to a place where we can 'ave
our desire."

Chedlowe bowed, staring at him. "I'll wait that long," he said, "if my temper lets me."

"And if mine does," M. de Champvallon added, with some sharpness of tone; whereupon his choleric rival stepped toward him fiercely. But by good fortune for both of them another truce was called. They might have fought; but the phlegmatic Lecky came in, bearing a tray. They saw bread, cheese, cold meats, claret and ale. A man's body will rule him ridiculously sometimes; the two hot young men were eye to eye when the servant entered; but those fighting eyes wandered and became ravenous. Absurdly, M. de Champvallon and Mr. Chedlowe, without uttering another word, walked straight to the table where Lecky placed the tray; in silence they seated themselves there, opposite to each other, began to eat and drink, and ate and drank until nothing was left of food or liquors. Then Mr. Chedlowe looked heavily upon his opponent and would have freshened the quarrel but could not, and neither could M. de Champvallon. They were two young gentlemen who could go long without slumber but not forever, and they had not slept since they woke upon the Tuesday morning, and this was Thursday noontime. Now they had fed and they had drunk and were drugged within them.

Mr. Chedlowe rose, went sluggishly to the settle at the right of the fire and sat down there, his head back against the brown old wood. M. de Champvallon, having finished the last of the wine, got up with a look of brightness, went quickly to the settle at the left of the fire, seated himself gracefully, leaned back and, for a moment, regarded his vis-à-vis with an expression of amused contempt. Mr. Chedlowe resented this look; he frowned and said, "Tush, Frenchman!" But his eyes were closed when he spoke. M. de Champvallon, on his part, had no resentment for the "Tush, Frenchman!" His eyelids had closed while Mr. Chedlowe's were drooping.

CHAPTER IV

OUT on the clouded moorland, meanwhile, a young lady rode slowly upon
a fine white horse that limped. A person of some
talent, M. de Grammont, had made for an interested friend a verbal portrait of her, stressing the
opulent fairness of her hair, the pretty slyness of
her eyes and the richness of her figure; more than
hinting, too, that for the glamouring of gentlemen she counted upon these gifts of nature as a
balance to be set against sallowness and some
oddity of feature. M. de Grammont had omitted
two details of note: that the eyes were hazel,

most harmonious with the hair, and that seen in a crowd of prettier faces hers would have fixed an observer's eye the longest. Once looked at, moreover, she must be looked at again, and with puzzling in the looker, who would say to himself, "What strange thing is she thinking?" and get no answer, yet must go on questing for one.

On Wanton Mally she showed as the too hasty transplantation of a fine London dame to a dismal waste. Her wide velvet hat brim, the color of a light sherry, so drooped with the wet that it flapped down against her blonde hair that still held to some of its curling and its fashion of being worn like the drooping ears of King Charles's spaniels. Her dress, broadly open from the neck and breast and with sleeves ending in lace upon the upper arm, was of sherry-colored silk luxuriantly slashed and embroidered with pale green. Her velvet shoes, sherry-colored, too, and heeled with three inches of gilded leather, showed gold rose buckles seeded with pearls against pale green stockings; there was a brooch of pearls upon her breast, and, about her throat, a close necklace of

pearls that would have bought from Mr. Brunnage his manor of Mally Surfeit five times over.
It may be told, too, in the hope of shedding more
light upon her, that she had, invisible in the top
of her left stocking, a slim black silk purse that
had belonged to Bishop Bourne; but this she kept
not for the money in it but as a trophy, and one
to be held to all the more, the more risk there
was to keep it.

Earlier in the morning she had been aware of
voices in the fog, of hailings, hoarse commands
and bellowed responses, and, thus warned, she
often left the faintly traced path; then returned
to it warily. Often, too, she halted to listen, and
once heard voices startlingly near her using harsh
words about the weather and a thorn thicket.
She waited until these voices grumbled less perilously close to her, and, when she went softly forward again, found that her horse began to limp.
Thenceforward there was nothing for it but to
let him walk at his own lame gait; and thus tard-
ily, yet always craftily, she drew toward the
trysting place she had appointed. But when at

last she came near the juncture of the road and the two paths, she bore away and approached the thatched house from its other side.

All was somewhat sourly familiar to her here; she rode into a stable doorway, saw there a black horse and a bay horse and Lecky, and dismounted. Lecky looked at her hard; then touched his thicket of tow hair with a forefinger but said nothing.

"He's within?" she asked, in her husky voice.

"Ma'am, he's been to London these ten days but said when he left he'd be home to-night."

"To London, has he?" she said, staring suddenly. "Two to go and two to come; he would have been in the town six days, then." She had her own thoughts here, expressed them by a visibly quickened breathing, then looked at the bay horse and the black horse, and asked, "Where are your two visitors?"

"In the hall, asleep."

"Let them stay so. Rub Snow's off fore fetlock with hot vinegar and bind it with tight cloths before he feeds." She went to a door that gave access to a narrow covered passageway to the house; but paused and glanced back over her shoulder. "You do look for him by nightfall?"

"Ay; but he might come afore."

"Ay," she said, in a muttering voice not amiable. "He might do anything." Then, striding, head up, she went through the passageway and came into the kitchen, where she suddenly stood still and put a hand to her side as if what she saw brought hurt to her there; but her eyes were angry. "Fut!" she said, and went to searching the cupboards; for her hunger was as sharp as had been that of the fugitive gentlemen. She ate and drank zestfully until she had no room for more, and what had happened to them happened also, in the course of nature, to herself. Her eyelids became languorous, like the eyelids Mr. Lely had painted in his portrait of her; she rose rustily, walked through the bare bedroom beyond the kitchen as if she dragged herself, opened the farther door and looked dreamily into the hall.

Upon the floor between the settles there was a clutter, two plumed big hats, two swords and sword-belts, dropped for the greater ease of the two collapsed figures that slumbered upon the settles and were lighted pinkishly upon one side, toward the comforting fire, and greyly upon the other, toward the vapored windows. Mistress Jinny Wilmot said "Fut!" again but with no spirit, her voice smothering under drowsiness; and turned back to the bed. She bent toward it but shivered and with a flicker of energy pulled forth the tick stuffed with feathers and dragged this into the hall, where she kicked her two friends' accoutrements aside and made place for it between the settles; then she dropped her big hat upon that of M. de Champvallon and herself, in the same instant, upon the feather-bed before the fire. Once down, she stirred with a languid shivering; then felt the soothing warmth of the fire, and moved no more than a fallen statue. From time to time Mr. Chedlowe snored lightly, disturbing the peace of the scene not a whit.

This hall in the humble house of Mr. Colpoys was then wholly at peace. With its three slumbering figures before the fire, and the silence of the Wanton Mally fog all round about, it might have been thought the safest haven in the isles.

CHAPTER V

ELSEWHERE upon Wanton Mally there could easily have been a different opinion. By noon Mr. Brunnage had passed through Colonel Bourne's scattered soldiers without seeing a man of them; two hours later he was at Littlefield but there turned back upon the moor, and, after a time, came by accident smack upon the Colonel. This brother to the Bishop was a giant-like black-chinned brown man, all leather and steel, and now, when Brunnage found him, full of vengeance perilously bottled. In spite of his episcopal kinship he swore pro-

fanely, filling the Justice's ears with wicked
sound not uncongenial to them. "Do ye have fog
everlasting in these parts?" he asked in conclu-
sion. "A regiment could 'a' gone through us ten
times over or passed you and your louts on the
other side, so where's my three bloody rogues?
Off the moor through you or back through me
and on their way to London, laughing at both of
us?"

"Nay, nay!" Mr. Brunnage cried, and wagged
his head cunningly. "Leave it to me, Col'nel
Bourne; they're not off Wanton Mally and I'll
lay my hand on 'em heavy enough in good time."

" 'In good time'! When's that to be?"

"It might be," said Mr. Brunnage coolly, "it
might be as late as this night; but by certainty
before midnight, unless they be late on the road."

"On what road?"

"Ah, when I say the road," Mr. Brunnage explained, "I mean whatever way they take. They
may be sly and wriggle over the moor deviously
on no road or path. What bodes it how they
come, or by what way, if a body knows what
hole they make for?"

Colonel Bourne was a trooper and again swore like one. This is an old comparison and may have been born in the travail of some decent soul acquainted with the Colonel. When he was coherent, "What body knows that?" he asked. "What hole? What hole?"

"Looky," Mr. Brunnage said. "You know of a house called Mally Older here on the moor?"

"I? How should I? Was I ever in this devil's weed-patch till to-day? I was not! The landlord at Littlefield told me how to get a message to you, or I'd not had you out. What of this Mally Older?"

"This," Mr. Brunnage said. "It's a house owned and lived in these three year by one Tom Colpoys. Now looky, Col'nel Bourne; from his first coming I had suspicion of him as a hard rogue, for it was known he was of London and kept loose company there. Why should such a fancy man, one with store o' goods and money, too, why should such a fellow hide himself in a plain house deep in this moor? Why doth he avoid all folk hereabouts and when he journeys let no man know his errand? There you have it; I

say a fellow that leads a hidden life hath ill cause
for't and 's one to be watched. Now what d'you
say to this? The twelvemonth past or something
more he's been almost provenly known for a
Quaker! Quakers, male and female, that was
looked for by the law, he's believed to have hid
in his house and spirited on to other parts as if
they vanished."

"Ah, so?" Colonel Bourne said, and made plain
his strong conviction that the King was too
sweet-hearted. The gaols were full of Quakers
who died there peacefully instead of being hanged
and so handed over suitably to the brimstone tor-
ments that pined to receive the traitorous here-
tics. Returning from the general to the individ-
ual, however, "What o' this Colpoys o' yours?"
the Colonel asked. "He hides here, you say, and
that's ill; he's a Quaker and hides Quakers, and
that's worse. But do you hint he had to do with
a Quaker plot against my brother?"

"Trust me, I'll do more than hint," Mr. Brunnage said, frowning under pressure of his heavy
suspicions, and straightway fulfilled his promise. The Justice and the Colonel were men of like

conviction; they were of the staunch, pig-headed stock that again was to make England sturdy. To their minds church and state were a twin-ship; in England there could be but one church, as there could be but one state, and whoever denied this was abhorrent. The Justice and the Colonel mistrusted everything they misunderstood, and, for England's and virtue's sake, would exterminate what they hated. Tithes were the life of the church and fealty of the subject was the life of the crown; the Quakers were traitors who banded together to mock at payment of tithes and bound themselves to refuse the Oath of Allegiance to the King, thus committing two crimes that struck most vitally at England's very self. In words that mortally offended any soldier and incensed judges and lawyers, they declared they would not bear arms for king and country, or for any cause; this made them hypocrite rebels, and who believed a rebel so sly would not strike when he could do it secretly? Who believed he would not trick himself out as a highwayman to murder a proper Quaker-baiting bishop in the dusk? Mr. Colpoys, owner of that long, thatched house of Mally Older, was indeed suspectible, and the Colonel, who loved church, state and his brother, the Bishop, leaned a hungry ear toward the Justice.

Mr. Brunnage made his case against the alleged Quaker even more damnatory than he had made it earlier in the day for his own benefit with M. de Grammont to the less eager ear of M. de Champvallon. All the while of his residence at Mally Older this Colpoys had engaged himself in secret employment, dangerous unknown readings and writings, it was well believed, Quaker plottings and the like. Ten days since, he had set off for London and would be at home this night, as had been discovered from his servant without giving the man anything unusual to think about. Now, Colpoys, travelling at a fair pace from London, would have been in the town at the hour of the foul assault: Why had he allowed himself just the time that would cover the deed and bring him easily home at the hour he'd appointed? And looky now, had not the Quakers threatened often that their punishers would be punished by strange means? And there was

Bishop Bourne, straight from preaching against 'em, attacked by clouded figures, one most strangely a woman. What! Where could be any doubt in a shrewd mind? Nay, nay! Look for Colpoys and a male and a female Quaker with him! The thing was fixed in the Justice's mind and became almost as well set into the Colonel's.

He swore by all he worshipped and by the organs of life within him that this black-hearted Colpoys would be looked to suddenly. "And by my blood, I think you have the rights of it, Brunnage! We'll ride straightway for this Mally Older!"

"Soft, soft!" Mr. Brunnage said. "That might be to warn my two dog-foxes and the vixen. We know they're on the moor because they passed out on it from Littlefield, so—"

"They're on it, stab my liver! We know they're on it but—"

"Better still, we know they can't be off it, Col'nel. They couldn't cross it afore midday when the folk all around about its landward edges be roused in arms and set to get wind of 'em. On the other side, the sea's our guard, and did we drive 'em there they'd be gulled, for they must needs turn gull to be away on that lonely side o' Wanton Mally." Mr. Brunnage thought well of his wit, took the time to laugh unctuously at the jest he'd made; then confidently began to explain plans he'd formed for the capture. "Now looky! They'll be wary how they go to earth, and if we be in their hole when they come nigh it they'll turn back or run off to one side or the other and haply make the chase more wearisome for us. Colpoys knows Wanton Mally like the room he sleeps in, and be sure he'll come watchfully to Mally Older, and not afore the dark, sith he's said he'll be there then and will reason an he come sooner some might learn of it and wonder that he rode so fast from London-town."

"Ay, they might!" the Colonel agreed. "How saddle-sore d'you think we are, me and my fellows?"

"No doubt, no doubt; but henceforth ye'll all be easier, Col'nel. We'll ride easy, and my plan'll take Colpoys without hazard of losing him. If we catch him on the moor, that is well—we'll go on seeking him as we beat towards Mally Older

in comfort—but where we be sure of him is
there at his house when the dusk falls, which'll
be early, in the fog. Let him be in his hole before
we go into it."

"I swear," the Colonel began, and proved himself truthful. "We'll out-cunning our beast and
catch him as you say, Brunnage. We'll make this
Mally Older the middle of our net. Lead us that
way, creeping, and I'll weave my dozen fellows
into the meshes for him. Any fish shall go in but
not out. I give you praise, Brunnage. I must
hale the three foul hearts back to London for
trial there; but if 'twas left to me I'd truss 'em
to three stakes and burn 'em out o' hand this
night on your proofs against 'em."

"You shall have better," Mr. Brunnage promised. "You shall find proof enough to sate you in
the stables at Mally Older, Col'nel Bourne!"

CHAPTER VI

ow it has never been an uncommon thing for three people to be riding together, or extraordinary that such a group should consist of one woman and two men. Nor would it be a miracle that two such groups should ride toward the same place on the same day; and, as for Tom Colpoys's having with him a couple, man and wife, riding privately to Mally Older, this was nothing unprecedented, for it was a thing that happened with even some regularity. Nevertheless, the circumstance that Colpoys, with a woman and a man, rode toward

Mally Older while Mrs. Jinny Wilmot, M. de
Champvallon and Rafe Chedlowe, having ridden
thither, lay sleeping there, might be thought
both singular and luckless, yet not enough of
either to be unparalleled. For a close likeness to
such a happening, however, archives must be
searched; and, being examined, they yield up
the case of the Clement Shepherd and the Devil's
Widow, a process once notorious.

It was in the North and in a time remembered
by the grandsires of men who were still alive
when King Charles's grandsire began to reign.
A great part of the North had a contagion of
worrying about the Devil; the fear of him was in
all hearts and could not be put away, so that any
poor cotter's family, like the Lord in his Hall,
felt Beelzebub imminent upon the threshold with
the falling of every dusk. Night and day there
was gossiping of him, of his habits and horrid
trickiness, and he was known to be walking
abroad in the land, wearing the air and looks of
a persuasive man. At Breaklets, a town the most
fear-ridden, there was a chirurgeon known to
be full of science, and he said that if this pre-

tended man could be held long enough for the liver to be had out of him and burned, the Devil's soul would return to its proper home in the heat below ground, but happily without its mind. Thus the Devil, having no intelligence, would by all decent logic possess no guile, and so could trouble living people little thereafter. Near this same Breaklets a shepherd fell asleep among his flock and dreamed that the Devil came to Breaklets in company with a Minor Demon; in this dream the Devil was dressed in brown and appeared like a talkative man of middle-age, while the Minor Demon wore the guise of a sulky youth who led a donkey that bore a pack of merchandise. Then, waking, the shepherd ran to Breaklets, declared his dream and asked to be placed, with pay for his time, near the town gates so that he could identify Old Scratch and help to get his liver if he risked coming there.

For a time the shepherd's dream proved of no avail, and there was talk of annulling his new office, when upon a noontime he began to shriek and pointed toward the gates. There, entering the town, were a man, a youth and a pack-donkey. The man's garments were of blue cloth; but he was of middle-age and wore a brown hood, and, what was even more sinister, he talked briskly to the youth beside him—that is to say, he did so until the townsfolk ran to heap themselves upon him and his attendant. Soon indeed he said nothing and wore nothing, and the Minor Demon fared no better, though the donkey was spared and became the joint reward of the shepherd and the chirurgeon. Later there was a little time of embarrassment, for a widow of Sussex came, complaining of the loss of a husband and his apprentice, travelling merchants. She brought suit against the shepherd, the chirurgeon, a sheriff and a constable, the four who'd shown the greatest zeal in destroying satanic seats of the mind, and she hoped at least to have the donkey back from the shepherd and the chirurgeon, and the merchandise from the sheriff and the constable; but the action was settled more creditably for Breaklets, and in the end she was sent to prison for contumacy, and the fine new tavern

in the town was gratefully named and ever thereafter known as the Clement Shepherd.

So in the affair of Thomas Colpoys, it must be
Mr. Brunnage who plays this part of the Clement
Shepherd, and the parallel holds closely here, for
though Mr. Brunnage was an honest man and
earnest in his suspicions, like the shepherd, he
may have had the tail of his eye on Mally Older,
where sheep might be made to pay. The Devil
at Breaklets had brown on his head only but it
cost him dear; Mr. Brunnage was at least more
legal-minded than the shepherd and might have
had his prejudice somewhat baffled had he come
upon Tom Colpoys riding a bay horse and the
woman with Colpoys upon a bay, and the man
likewise upon a bay. These three, in fact, all rode
bays, wore cloaks not black, and their clean faces
showed no faintest trace of soot. They rode in
a pleasant manner, moreover, holding cheerful
talk together, and had no apprehensions roused
by mischievous consciences.

The owner of Mally Older was a thin-faced,
long gentleman but easy in his motions and
strongly shaped; what a thinking stranger first

considered was the hazel twinkling of his eyes. His look seemed to put forth about him a sort of troubled kindness, as if he intended benevolence toward the world but in respect to his opinion of himself sought a middle course between laughing and crying. He wore his own hair, tawny and uncurled but waving upon his shoulders, used plain linen instead of lace, had no feathers upon his big hat, and, for the rest, wore soft leather and fine dark cloth. Even the hilt of his sword, like the sheath, was a lack-luster grey; but, in spite of all this sobriety, he was near cutting a lively figure beside the dun-colored pair that rode with him.

Those two were warmly clothed but with a simplicity so strait as to betoken fervor. Both rode between packs fastened before and behind their saddles as if in provision for a longer journey than one to Mally Older, and there was something of expectancy of such a journey, too, in their faces. The man was small, dark and eager-looking; the woman, about twenty-four, of a startling, pale beauty. Her husband's cousin, of Cambridge, a farrier's son getting knowledge

beyond his station, had written a poem about
her, saying that her eyes did glister with the July
noonday blue and that her hair and brows were
with golden stardust spangled. She had a face
that for a fact shone starrily with bright mild-
ness in the fog, both her husband and Mr. Colpoys thought—yet she was only the wife of a
little Wiltshire tanner. Her very name indeed,
since marriage, came from her husband's business, a matter he explained as the three bay
horses drew together again upon issuing from a
ravine. This party had not come by Littlefield;
Mr. Colpoys took a shorter way to Wanton
Mally, and, upon the moor, followed no path
visible at all. The Colonel and the Justice and
their people ranged the while some miles to the
southward.

"The name came from the work and it could
be thought the work came from the name, too,"
the husband said. "Tanners and workers in
leather since time out o' mind we've been; so
that, bearing the name, a grandson thought tanner he must be, since he was sure to be called one
because his grandsire'd been one. I'd 'a' felt more

down in heart when I said farewell to my old tanning-yard, Monday night, had I not thought of how I carried the name upon me and the trade itself with me in my head, and so in a manner shall never wander from the tannery."

"Nor from a living either," Colpoys said. "Where men go shod and belted there must be tanning, and who carries in his head a necessary trade is safer in this world, I think, than him with only money in his purse. You have the better of me there, Francis."

"Why, no," Francis Tanner responded. "I think there's more money in thy purse than trade in my head, friend."

"Well, matters could be worse with me perhaps," Colpoys assented. "So long as the money keeps to the level of my purse I may do well enough; but I knew many in London whose money had risen to their heads—they couldn't speak without jingling." He smiled at Master Francis's wife. "You're content with a husband that does more thinking than jingling, aren't you, Anne?"

"I am," she said, and looked at Colpoys with

a timidity that had wistfulness in it, as if she thought about him with deference and anxiety commingled. "Was it the jingling alone that turned thee away from London?"

"No; that had little to do with my coming to Wanton Mally."

"Then what——" she began; but paused, and, at the cost of exposing a gentle hardihood, went on, "All our talk with thee bends upon my husband and me. It could not help but be so while he and I stood in harm's way. While we were threatened, I fear our minds were upon little but the soreness of the threat. From the first of thy coming to us we've talked of ourselves, our plight, thy plan for us—and then of ourselves again!" She laughed as if shyly to beg from his amiability an excuse for her intrusion. "I thought of this last night when we lay under the yew tree. I thought, 'To-morrow we'll be so much nearer safety we can forget ourselves a little, my husband and I—perhaps we can speak of our friend and he'll speak more of himself.' Yet the hours go on and it does not come to pass. Isn't it time, friend?"

He shook his head ruefully. "I know what you
wish, Anne Tanner. You have a face that's no
better hiding-place for you than a glass casket.
You can't see a creature and not yearn to make
shine into him the light you see; so you reason if
you coax me to discourse of Tom Colpoys you
can seize upon this or that in his history and
show him how the true light would ease his
heart."

"Nay," she said. "That's not all."

Upon this he became graver, and, not asking
her to explain what more she meant, understood
her gratefully. "Have your way, lady. I'll give
you all the knowledge of me I can; but first, to
help you, I'll tell you of others like me as I was,
for I wasn't singular then and I'm not now, as
you see. No creature is singular, I believe, and,
when one in vanity thinks he is so, it is because
his gaze is too much upon himself, for if he look
about him he will see himself mocked by a great
number of his counterparts. No, we all have our
fellows as like to ourselves as the pups of a litter
to one another, and I think the most part of history is the quarrelling between such litters or

fellowships, the which litters or fellowships or peas in the pod seem willed to repeat themselves and their quarrels again and again in every age through eternity. Your own fellowship, Anne, was known by the ancient Romans; I speak of the martyrs and saints."

She laughed. "I never heard that they ran away. I thought thou'd speak of—"

"Of me! I do; but you'll find me a great talker on that or any subject, made so by solitude and vanity working together. Two of my litter-brothers, with markings like mine, have been men of broad ill-repute—my lord of Rochester that you know of, and the third king of France before this present Lewis. You may call them penitents debauched or devils repentant or mad-men, as you choose; they had a time for doing evil and a time for most horrid remorse—they would live so many months in poison and corruption and so many weeks thereafter in prayer and flagellation. So did I."

"Truly?" she asked, and smiled placidly. "How long ago?"

"Until three years ago. I kept my habits of

repentance private from my friends in town, and
I should tell you that the times of pure behavior
were of the shortest and rose in great part from
fever of the head when I'd been too long merry
with those friends. While I was merry, always
tolerably in wine, I thought myself no worse
than merry and my companions merry sweet
fellows and the world a merry meadow for frolic.
Then when I was penitential I took horse and
rode out of the town to find places as lonely as
I could for the best escape from everything but
the one worst thing—the which was the fellow
I hated most and had most with me when I was
most alone. Then after some hard nights and
days of goodness I'd be jogging back towards the
town anxious to be at my merry ways again; and
on such a jog, one day, it fell out that I saw folk
on a green listening to a man who spoke to them,
and I stopped and sat my horse to listen. There
were some near me that laughed, and, when I
asked them why they did so, they told me the
folk were Quakers and the man was George
Fox."

Anne Tanner's breathing paused for a mo-

ment, and her husband uttered a sound of exclamation. "Thou'st seen him, then! Thou'st
looked upon George Fox!"

"Seen him and heard him," Colpoys answered.
"I had no speech with him; but I felt what is
told of the power of his eyes, for they seemed
to search out every face about him, and, as I sat
higher than the others on my horse, I thought
he looked more than once at me. Indeed he
seemed to speak to me, which I make no doubt
all felt—that he spoke to every man singly."

"And the light?" Anne asked with wonder.
"It did not come to thee then?"

Colpoys shook his head. "No; but something
did. I knew nothing of the Friends; I'd heard
them bawled at as 'Quakers', and, like all of my
acquaintance, I took them to be what they're
reputed—a contumacious sect, leagued for mis-
chief to everything of established worth in the
land. Well, I listened to George Fox and knew it
wasn't so; when I first saw his face I knew it
could not be so, for this was a man of an extraordinary great spirit for kindness. What he said
was said to strengthen the poor folk about him

in unresentment of wrong done upon them, and when he'd gone I stayed for talk with some who'd stood closest about him, and I asked them to tell me of him and somewhat of themselves. They were as contumacious as doves and as like to do harm! I stayed there among them for a month, and I tell you this of George Fox: before I had stopped seeing and hearing him, that day, I knew I would not go back to my old ways in the town."

"But if thou'd gone to London then," Anne said, "it would have been to no ill. Thou'd have brought thy companions there into better ways."

"My companions there!" Colpoys murmured, and looked compassionate for her innocence. "My dear, I am no dealer in thunderbolts and miracles; my own ways were enough for me to better! After the month I rode away but not towards London. Those Quakers had set up a mortal disturbance in me; but I couldn't live by the light they kept upon their actions. For one barrier, I knew I could never be mishandled and abide it; but in all things I was perplexed. I couldn't make head nor tail of this world or our life in it, and, when it chanced that riding on and on I came upon this wild moor of Wanton Mally, I thought I was at last in a place I was befitted for, so, after a time, I began to live in the old, sorry house where you're to lie this night, for I thought that Wanton Mally was like the world, a bewilderment and a waste, but better for me to dwell in. Well, whatsoever world a man finds about him, he must do something more than think, and, when I had thought until I was more fusty-headed than when I began, I was listless on the moor, one day of fog like this, and the place itself, being what you see it, seemed to tell me on a sudden what I should do."

The tanner's wife inclined her head in a serious corroboration. "Yes. When the spirit's anguished, light seems to come upon it from something without—might appear to shine from a tree or the wall of a cell, or a voice might seem to speak from a cloud. What was it thy spirit made clear to thee?"

"I can't say it was my spirit," he said. "Yet it's true I knew on a sudden how to busy myself with something better than either roistering or moping. Many, many of those kind poor folk, the Friends, withered in prison, and more would soon let themselves lie withering there; for when they were persecuted they wouldn't avail themselves of any means to avoid the cruelties done upon them. My thought was to go among such as I knew, and others they'd tell me of, and persuade those most threatened, if I could, how to keep their faith and yet spare themselves such suffering as I could show them to be useless. What you say my spirit made clear to me, Anne, was how to be a friend to Friends, even though I couldn't be a Friend myself."

"But the step to be one is so short," the little tanner urged hopefully. "Almost thou'rt wholly of us. Thou could be one, friend; thou could be one."

"No; not now, and not then. A man can be proclaimed a king and be one; but his spirit cannot be made what it is not by any proclamation nor by any profession of his own."

"When Wanton Mally seemed to speak that message," Anne asked, "it brought the plan, too, with it?"

"It did. I went privately to her Grace of Portsmouth with whom I had a small acquaintance, enough to know her willingness towards gift-taking, and so I had the grant of the tract of land you know of across the sea. I bought also the little ship, the 'Hopeful', and had her brought to the bay beyond Wanton Water. Then I went again among those Friends I'd visited; spoke to those threatened with writs, as I did to you yesterday, showing them how they could live to better service in new lands than in old gaols. So I took such of them as I'd persuaded to Mally Older and thence to sail upon the 'Hopeful'. I brought them by the very way we've come to-day and they went on by the way we'll go to-morrow with none the wiser. They were the first and they were nine; but since then there have been upwards of nine score. Many, too, have gone openly by the 'Hopeful', enough to make great need for a man of your skill in the arts of tannery and leather-working, Francis. If so be there's a fair voyage I think all else is fair before you, too."

"And already we're sure to make the voyage

without hindrance?" the tanner asked confidently.

"Yes, since our nags first set hoof on Wanton Mally. From Mally Older it's not twelve miles to where the 'Hopeful' will drop anchor at dawn, and to-morrow we'll rise betimes to set you aboard of her close on sun-up."

"Mally Older," Anne said, murmuring the name as if it pleased her. "We'll be there by dark, belike?"

"By dark?" Colpoys said, and, looking up into the thickness above him as if he sought the hidden sun, he laughed. "Well past noon now, I think, and dark enough; but without this fog you could see the three chimneys of Mally Older. We're not a mile from there."

CHAPTER VII

SINCE all men dream continually while they sleep, the Chevalier de Champvallon, inert upon his settle at Mally Older, must have been dreaming for something more than three hours before his slumber grew light enough to form those shimmering edges remembered by an awakened sleeper as dreams. He found himself where he had been more than once, in battle, with muskets crackling about him, and, at the same time, he had a faint belief that somebody had been heartening a dull fire with new wood. The Chevalier had eyelashes so noticeable that the protection of their honor was the cause of a deep scar on his left fifth rib; flickering a little now, they let him believe he looked upon a twinkling heap of amber and pale emeralds. The fringes parted more widely and he became fitfully aware of a rich shape of sherry color and light green rosily glowed upon below him. Then he saw a still cascade of white gold spilling over the edge of the mattress where Jinny lay face downward, her forehead upon her wrist, and, comprehending, he sighed in drowsy approval, and would have slept again. Something kept his eyes from closing quite; he felt perturbance, and, looking slowly upward, saw that the door of the bedroom between hall and kitchen was partly open, that a man's head and one shoulder were in the aperture and that the man was gazing at him. The gaze was thoughtful and the face disturbing—that is to say, it was a face disturbing to M. de Champvallon, for he took it to be that of Mr. Colpoys, as it was, and he felt immediately that owned by a rival such a face might be troublesome to even a gentleman highly practised at Versailles in wooing.

The head and shoulders withdrew and the door closed. M. de Champvallon looked down again at the firelit figure upon the mattress, and pondered a while; then all at once alert he rose, went lightly to the door, opened it, passed through the bare bedchamber and made his appearance smilingly in the kitchen. There was a fire here, too, now and cooking had been done. The master of Mally Older sat at table with a woman whose comeliness twice warmed the young Frenchman's heart, once on beauty's own account and again because it is in company with such charms that a lover loves to see a rival. M. de Champvallon bowed eloquently to Anne Tanner and elegantly to his host. "Madame!" he said. "Sir! I beg every excuse for myself. My name is de Champvallon and I am a traveller brought 'ere by a frien' of Misterr Colpoys. I speak to Misterr Colpoys?"

"Sir, you do."

M. de Champvallon bowed again, and kept a seemingly careless eye upon his host's expression. "Earlier in the day I was alone and could not find my way; but a gentleman show' me mercy and did tell me. 'E said 'is name was Bron-age."

"So? He was near here when you spoke with him?" Colpoys asked; but the Chevalier observed that his look, like his tone, seemed unconcerned.

"No, not very near. 'E was riding the other way from 'ere and 'e was thinking 'e would meet somebody else." M. de Champvallon spoke more slowly. " 'E tol' me 'e thought there were bad people that wish to 'ide themselves upon Vanton Mallee."

"So?" Tom Colpoys's tone was easy and uninterested; but Anne stared blankly at the young Frenchman.

"Bad—people?" she murmured.

"To Brunnage all people are somewhat wicked," Colpoys said, and laughed cheerfully. "All but himself. Lecky tells me Brunnage has suspicion of every man at Mally Surfeit to be a thief that he doesn't already know for a poacher. What kind of ill fellows did he look for this morning, Monsieur de Champvallon?"

M. de Champvallon smiled vaguely. "Ah, that I cannot say; but 'e was sure 'e would catch

somebody." Then he appeared to toss Mr. Brunnage aside with a change of subject. "But you are
from a journey; I fear Madame Colpoys 'as been
very col' to ride so far in this naughty fog."

"Madame Colpoys?" his host repeated inquir-
ingly; but Anne, recovered from her blankness,
laughed.

"That's a great flattery to me," she said. "My
husband's had his dinner and is gone to be of use
in the stables. That rejoices him," she went on,
smiling to Colpoys. "He never rode a fine horse
till yesterday and now he has six to pleasure his
eyes withal."

"Six fine 'orses!" M. de Champvallon exclaimed indulgently, and seemed to pleasure his
own eyes with the lady before him. "It make'
your 'usban' 'appy to look at 'orses? A black
'orse, a bay 'orse, a pale 'orse and—" He laughed.
"But I do not know the color of the other three
'orses."

"All bay and beautiful," Anne told him, nodding. "Three splendid bay horses of friend Colpoys's."

"Ah, three bay? 'Ow pretty!" For a moment

he seemed to muse upon this prettiness, then to remind himself of a duty. "But I mus' make my excuse that I address' you as Madame Colpoys, Madame. Also I mus' not be a such selfish fellow that will keep you 'ere in talk when per'aps you wish repose after the long ride in the damp?"

"No, no," she said, for she had never seen his like nor ever before had speech with a Frenchman, and was childishly pleased with him. "I'm not wearied—unless friend Colpoys wishes to speak alone with—"

This time the Chevalier observed her manner of referring to the owner of the house, and seemed enchanted with it. "No, no; there are no secrecies—but 'ow pleasantly you employ a word! I mus' remember it and try to deserve it of some kind lady of France when I return there. As you speak it, Madame, it signify as if you say, 'A such man is brother to me, a such man is 'usban' to me; but Misterr Colpoys is frien' to me—he hol' that office.' It is very pretty!"

"But—" Anne began; then, as she caught a glance from Colpoys, withheld explanation.

"Pretty!" M. de Champvallon repeated, with

gay approval. "A very pretty thing to remember!" He was sincere in his appreciation, and
indeed all of this little episode appeared to him as
pretty: the firelight playing upon the glass and
dishes of the finished meal where sat a gentleman
beside a lady whose loveliness no dun disguise
could darken—and the husband affably where he
should be, interesting himself in horses! More,
the scene was so much to the Chevalier's taste
that he wished others might behold it with him,
and, if one other in particular should come so
to behold it, he felt that more than one good
purpose would be served. "I retire," he said. "I
mus' not make myself welcome too long", and
thereupon he bowed so spaciously and swept his
hand to his heart in a gesture so elaborate that
in the same moment he knocked over a chair
behind him and upset a tall empty bottle that
stood near the edge of the table. The chair
thumped heavily, the bottle broke loudly upon
the floor, M. de Champvallon shouted "Dolt!"
furiously at himself, and made more noise with
his efforts to avert both of these accomplished
catastrophes. "Dolt! Dolt! Dolt!" he shouted,

berating himself. "I beg a hundred pardon', I beg a thousan', I beg ten thousan'! What do I make you think of Frenchmen! I beg you to belief the mos' maladroit of all my race now stan' before you! What can I say? What can I do to prove my penitence for a such——"

"No need, no need," Colpoys said, astonished by so much protestation. "There is no damage done. Nothing's the worse, Monsieur de Champ-vallon. Nothing——" He paused, looking toward the doorway, which the Chevalier had left open behind him upon his entrance.

Quick feet came from the hall and through the bedchamber; a husky voice said "Ha!" before its owner reached the doorway. Then Jinny Wilmot crossed the threshold, took one stride into the room, brought her feet together and stood still, looking fiercely at Anne Tanner. She lifted an arm and pointed at Anne. "Who's that?" she said. "Who's that?"

This hot abruptness, this hurling out of all that should be mannerly, left Mr. Colpoys as little able to reply as it did the tanner's gentle wife. They had risen but only to stare, it seemed,

They had risen in confusion.

"Who's that?"

in a motionless kind of confusion that the impetuous lady facing them thought significant enough. "Why—you—" she said, with a muffled articulation. Then, to the eyes of M. de Champvallon, she seemed a woman all ablaze, but with more than the firelight. She strode straight to Colpoys and struck him hard upon the mouth with her clinched hand. "You liar!" she cried.

Upon that, there was a hushed sort of tumult of three voices in the room. Anne made little outcries diminishing in loudness; Colpoys murmured, "Jinny! Jinny! Jinny!" over and over, helplessly, and with a kerchief patted a lip cut by a diamond; M. de Champvallon, almost with tears of admiration and pain, said, "Glorieuse! Hélas, you feel so much for 'im?"

But the voice of the attacking lady whipped above these others; she kept her face close to that of Colpoys. "How many years have you lied to me! You must stay in the wilderness to meditate, must you? Ah, you sorry, sorry liar! No place for Jinny Wilmot here! Out upon her and out with her! 'No! No! She harms my soul; she can't be here and I'll not go back with her, for I must be alone to think! Out with you, Jinny! Back to London with you, Jinny! Give me peace of you, Jinny, peace to be alone!' Alone! Ah, you wretch, you wretch!"

She said more, cursing him for a traitor to her, and was so sacrilegious and so outspoken that the Quakeress, trembling and red, ran to the door to the passageway. "I'll go to my husband," she said; but Jinny, leaving Colpoys, flung herself at the door and would not let her.

"Boh! Boh! So you keep husbands with you, too, do you? Why, here's a very slough of wickedness!"

"No, Madam," Anne said breathlessly, in agitation forgetting the Friends' manner of speech. "There's no wickedness here unless 'tis yours, Madam."

" 'Madam'! 'Madam'!" Jinny cried, and showed the fury a jealous blonde woman feels for only another as fair. " 'Madam' not me, wench!" But Colpoys caught the hand that rose to strike the tanner's wife as it had struck himself.

"Out, Anne," he said, and held Jinny fast while Anne slipped through the doorway.

Jinny kicked him upon the knees. "Let be! Let be! Let be!"

Colpoys lifted her, carried her a little way from the door and set her down with her face toward the opposite wall. "Nay, I'll go, too," he said, strode back and shut the door, with himself in the passageway beyond it. She threw herself at the door as he rang the bolt on its farther side; she kicked the lower panels and beat the upper with her fists.

"Dear child," M. de Champvallon besought her, in a sad voice, "repose yourself. 'E will not go far."

She turned, said scornfully, "Oh, you!" and ran toward the other door, that of the bedchamber, to go out through the hall; but he placed himself in her way and stopped her.

"Dear child! My word of honor 'e will not go far."

"Why not?"

"Dear Jeeny, I will tell you if you will 'ave a little patience to—"

"Patience! Patience! Have you turned to preaching, Champvallon?" But she seemed unconcerned with his answer, swung away from him and began to walk up and down the room. "What's it to me where that man goes? What's it to me whether he goes far or near or's in his house or out of it?"

"No?" the Chevalier said politely. "One moment ago it did seem something to you—a little? Yes, per'aps?"

"What!" she cried, and breathed fast, swinging her arms as she walked. "He's brought to an end with me now for his life long, I tell you! You don't believe me? Why, I'll have him killed if he comes to London again, but only to keep him from my sight so I'll not need be at the pains to look at him. Ha, he has a sore lip to be looked at; by heaven's mercy, I gave him that! Did you see?"

"See!" M. de Champvallon exclaimed lamentingly. "It was I who 'ad that dolorous stroke straight into my 'eart. My 'eart bled more than the lip of Misterr Colpoys."

"Your heart?" she said ruthlessly. "What's *your* heart to do with it?"

He bowed, as in apology. "Well, for me—for only me, I confess—everything! I think I resemble you a little. Your own 'eart did seem to mean something to you when you find that gentleman 'ere with a pretty lady? I think yes, per'aps a little! So mine was compel' to bleed. I beg you to pardon me if I speak of a such matter now; but when we ride away after our pleasantry with that poor Bishopp and I 'ad the honor to say to you that you were the mos' incomparable, astounding thing in the worl', I 'ad the belief that you turn' in your saddle and say to me, 'I love you'!"

"Well? Well?" Jinny said, without a pause in her pacing of the floor. Her brow and mouth expressed the annoyance of one who must deal with trifles in the moment of tragedy. "I said so. What of it? I am in love with you."

The Chevalier uttered a plaintive exclamation.

"Ah, love of ladies! She grant' me that ecstasy I would give my life for again and again; then she destroy me with the one stroke w'ich show me the truth. She tell' me she adore me and strike' another man so 'ard that he bleed!"

"I told you I was in love with you!" Jinny said angrily. "I am so. I've been in love with a dozen since that traitor left me, and now it's you. What more could you ask? I've ended with him wholly; I wish nothing of him but his life for the rogueries he practised on me! Ah, to think of the good will I had towards him, of the measures I took to find him and of my coming here to persuade him out of his hermitage! Oh, yes, he must be a hermit for his soul's sake, so he persuaded *me*. I was angry; but I went home and couldn't rest easy with the fear he'd gulled me for some tricksy dame bold enough when hidden here! I had such torment, oh, such shame! to think myself his gull. I travelled here to catch him, and each time found him at his old books and was almost gulled again; but not quite. He's not broke one pride I have left—that I didn't part with all suspicion of him! No, no, not all. So at

last I know what I was restless till I knew and
found him with his mud-haired cat!"

M. de Champvallon made gestures of despair.
"And she make' this oration to prove to me that
'er passion is for me! For my 'appiness she end'
with the confession that she bring me all the distance to Vanton Mallee in flight not to the safety
of our neck' but to discover Misterr Colpoys sitting beside a mud-'air' cat!"

Jinny halted and looked at him broodingly.
"You must have all my thoughts always upon
yourself, must you?"

"No; I could wish some of them some of the
time upon the safety of three neck', one of them
adorable."

"Pooh!" she said. "Aren't you safe enough?"

"I?" M. de Champvallon permitted his delicate smile to become a little emphasized. "I mus'
not reproach you for the failure to comprehen'
that a French gentleman with the safety of a
lady in 'is charge would be thinking of that and
not of 'is own."

"Pooh!" she said again. "My safety isn't in
your charge. Nor am I in your charge nor in any

man's. Do you forget who made Col'nel Bourne
lose us on the moor?"

The Chevalier shook his head indulgently.
"Dear child, I fear 'e 'as not los' us. I beg you
will listen—"

"Fut!" she said. "I may listen to you, once I've
done with Colpoys and his mud-cat."

"I knew! I knew!" M. de Champvallon cried.
"You love me so much you cannot listen to a
word from me till you 'ave struck 'im again!"

Mr. Chedlowe walked heavily into the room,
rubbing his eyes with his fist and smiling fondly
upon Mrs. Jinny. He had eaten and slept, and
now once more saw before him his heart's desire; he was a new man, a little drowsy but all
confidence. "I saw your hat and the feather-bed
and had joy in the sight," he said. "My mind was
troubled when you were not here; but now
you're with me again I'm ready for more sport.
When shall you and I begin to dupe this Bourne
again and squirm our way back to London?"

M. de Champvallon dropped into a chair and
looked at him earnestly. "Let me tell you of an
uncle of my mother's uncle," he said. " 'E was a

Huguenot and came to Paris with another Huguenot gentleman of Pau, the Marquis de Cirac, for the marriage òf King Henri with Madame Marguerite. They got very drunk together, very drunk, and one time they fell asleep in the cellar under a wine-shop. That night the massacre of all the Huguenots began, for it was the eve of Saint Bartholomew's day. The uproar all over the city woke up the uncle of my mother's uncle in the morning, and, through a little window at the top of the cellar wall, 'e saw the Huguenots being put to slaughter. So 'e sat down again beside M. de Cirac, and after a while the pistols and muskets and screaming woke up the Marquis de Cirac. 'Well! Well! Well!' M. de Cirac say to the uncle of my mother's uncle. 'From all the noise I think the wedding mus' be over, so now let us go and get our 'orses and ride back to Pau.' "

"Now, now!" Mr. Chedlowe protested impatiently. "What's the pother? What's all that about, Champvallon?"

"Nothing," M. de Champvallon said, with a light desperation. "Nothing excep' we 'ave as much chance to go 'ome as they did; and you, my poor Chedlowe, are the person, of all I ever know, who mos' make me think of the frien' of my mother's uncle's uncle, that Monsieur le Marquis de Cirac."

CHAPTER VIII

COLPOYS turned from the door he bolted and saw Anne Tanner, pale, leaning against the wall of the passage. "Will the dame come into her right senses again?" she whispered.

He shook his head. "It's not known whether or no she ever had them."

"What will she do?"

"That's not to be answered," he said. "As you saw, I once knew her very well; but never enough to know what she would do. I'm troubled that you—"

"Nay, nay," Anne interrupted, forestalling his

119

apology. "She did me no harm and I think Francis and I are in her debt."

"How could that be?"

"I may speak?" the Quakeress asked. "Friend, I think she was what turned thee towards the light."

"No; if I am turned towards it, which I doubt, my own misdoing—"

"Nay, but I think she had a part. There was the spirit in thee that was ashamed to see a woman so misgrown away from womankind and—"

"You think so?" Colpoys said, and laughed. "There's others of her kind in London, Anne— not like her, but of her kind."

"How strange! What kind are they? What do they think and do?"

"They think of their pleasure," he explained, indulgent with her bewilderment. "To get it they will do anything and endure anything. Why, like this Jinny's kinsman, Rochester, and like myself as I was, they will bear as much pain to get their pleasure as will honester folk to keep their religion, Anne."

"Then they do ill to themselves!" she cried softly. "Their pain's all pain; but ours is borne with joy. According to thee, a man can be made into a king by what is outward; but nothing outward hath strength to make his spirit into what it is not. Our religion is what our spirit knows and so will be kept with joy in the keeping. But for thy persuasion of us, Francis and I'd have been prisoned to-day where there's smallpox. Could that have made us unknow what we know, or not glad that we know it?"

"Not if you do know it," he said. "There are papists in gaol say the same, Anne. And those who put them there and would put you there believe they do it for that same good cause of knowing themselves in the right, though you Friends would prison none, and that's why I think you must be near the truth."

She looked aggrieved. "Near it! And thou did say the dame yonder would bear as much for her pleasure as we for—"

"I do think she would!" he said. "Her will to do what she will in her pleasure is her religion, and she will tear others and let herself be torn for it. So will all her kind, though not with so little ruth."

"Why will she?" Anne asked, and looked at him with a child-like, grave inquiry. "Why will she tear and be torn for the sake of pleasure?"

"It may be because she lives for this life alone and can see no other."

"Nay," Anne said. "I would live as I live if there was no other."

When she said this, he sighed and shook his head in regret that he had no such virtue. Then he said, "I could never find light enough to do that."

To his surprise she laughed. "But that's the light thou'st walked in these three years. More, thou'lt be of us soon. A little while ago I heard thee say mishandling could not be borne by thee without fighting, and now, so soon, I've seen thee struck cruelly upon the lips and suffer it peaceably."

"Oh, a woman—"

"I think she's more a man," Anne said, with a little sharpness. "They must be strange he-like creatures, these dames thou'st known in the town. What a time we live in and what a complexion of madness England bears, with its starving poor folk under all, and, above them, so many busy shouting, 'To prison with thee for not unknowing what thou knowest!' And then—on top of all—these perishers for pleasure! Is she now at Mally Older for her pleasure?"

The question came suddenly at Colpoys, though he had already asked it of himself and discovered no clear answer. "Not for her pleasure in teasing me, I think, as she's come before; and I am put to it to understand why she brought with her the French gentleman and Rafe Chedlowe."

"To help her do thee harm?"

"No; she would trust herself for that!"

"She will," Anne said quietly. "She will do thee what hurt she can and bring harm to Francis and me an she can."

"No; that she can't," he said, with more conviction in his voice than he had in his mind. "By sun-up to-morrow you and Francis shall be on the 'Hopeful'; but I think it may be we shouldn't sleep this night at Mally Older. I'll speak to Francis of it."

She smiled and touched his hand as they walked to the door at the end of the passage. "But we'll not speak to Francis of—of what she said. It is enough to tell him that she hath long borne thee ill will because she hath been slighted by thee."

"But that I never did," he said, with some simplicity. "I but stayed away from her. It will serve as well to tell Francis that she hates me without reason."

"Nay," Anne whispered, thus delaying his fingers upon the door-latch. "Francis and I know that none could hate thee with reason, and that none with reason could hate thee. Say that, being without reason, she hates thee."

"Well," Colpoys said, "I'll say she hates me."

This proved enough for their purpose. They found Francis engaged in the admiration of six horses that comfortably munched the fodder in their mangers; and he was not inquisitive. The bare statement that a woman hated his protector

was comprehensible to him without any imputa-
tion upon the gentleman; Master Tanner, all
good will himself, was yet too intelligent to
waste thought in rummaging for the origins of
ladies' mislikings. He was practical, too. "Well,
no matter how sore she hate thee, friend," he
said, "she can do thee no harm, nor Anne and
me neither, so long as she and her gentlemen
keep to the house here. If one of them rode away,
belike to lay an information before a Justice, we
could be more uneasy. If they lie here this night,
we'll be gone in their sleep and ride to where we
can wait for the ship's boat to take us up. Our
way's straight, isn't it?"

Colpoys agreed that it was and spoke as reassuringly; but presently, seeing Lecky outside,
went to him and drew him a little way from the
stables. "Squire Brunnage rode by this morning,
Lecky?"

"Ay. He had three from the Manor with him,
all four carrying arms. 'A stopped by the great
door and looked hard at the house; then Squire
kicked the door with his boot and stirrup, still
atop of his horse. I watched him from behind a

window; then went to ask his pleasure. 'Your master's not within?' I said you was not and he asked me, 'He's not yet home from London?' Then I bethought me when you went you said to look for you by this day dark, and I thought to say so openly would seem more open and careless; so I did."

"No fault of yours," Colpoys said, frowning. "When I went away, it was to send the ship openly from London with goods for our plantations and I had no thought I'd not come back to Mally Older alone. But from Friends in town I learned writs would be out for this Master Tanner and his wife at Biddesley; so I went there and showed them the need of the Friends on the plantations for a tanner and had their consent to go. But the cry was so loud against the poor souls I couldn't get them out but by this way. Did Brunnage say what he wished o' me or that he would come again?"

"He said, 'Well, no matter; another time, another time', and they rode away."

"As if to go back to Mally Surfeit?"

"T'other way, Master. 'A went on deeper in

the moor as if for Littlefield. I walked yonder towards the Mally and listened and knew that they stopped. The air in the fog was still so't I could hear 'em go on again; but one horse came back on the road, and I could hear a clinking and trotting, so't I knew Squire had sent back one of those with him, and I thought it might be this one had an errand to Mally Surfeit."

"It bears the look of it," Colpoys said musingly. "Brunnage was here asking of me, and when he knew I'd be here at nightfall he drew off, then sent a messenger back to Mally Surfeit."

"Ay, so 't was; but I thought it meant little, Master, and the message to have something he'd forgot brought to him, most like."

"Did the messenger come again this way as if to bring him something?"

Lecky rubbed his forehead. "Well, he might; but an he did I was out o' hearing. You're fretted by the matter, Master?"

"Not heavily, Lecky; but a little. Do you walk down the Mally—not far but so that if you hear horses you can run back and tell me before they're here."

"Ay, Master," Lecky said, and in a dozen strides was grey within the fog, while Colpoys stood thoughtful, his mind for the moment upon M. de Champvallon.

The young Frenchman had said that Brunnage looked for "bad people" upon the moor. Poachers slipping back to Littlefield, perhaps? No; M. de Champvallon had said that the "bad people" wished to hide themselves upon the moor. That, of course, might mean poachers from Mally Surfeit who dared not be found at home, and Brunnage might have stopped at Mally Older to ask Colpoys if perchance he'd seen lurkers anywhere; but if that were so why had not Brunnage asked such a question of Lecky? Moreover, why had the messenger been sent so soon after Brunnage knew that the owner of the house was not at home but would be by nightfall? Here was matter for uneasiness, at least: Brunnage astir and sure, almost, to be by this way on his return to Mally Surfeit—and Jinny Wilmot here ravening! Wanton Mally's ragged space waited hidden within the fog as to-morrow waits hidden within to-day. Monstrosity or nothing might come out of it, the one as easily as the other. Tom Colpoys had taken into his hands the safety of a man and a woman, both good and the woman sweet. He stared long at the vaporous mask, saw nothing, heard nothing, and found its expressionlessness disquieting.

CHAPTER IX

INDOORS was a mind disquieted like his for the safety of a woman, and, like his again, ready to go to any length—or perhaps any depth—for her preservation. A difference was that Colpoys saw a prison as the threat against his charge, while the danger pictured in the mind of the Chevalier de Champvallon was more hideous. Another difference, that the woman indoors could last of all be thought sweet, made no difference at all in M. de Champvallon's anxiety for her; he was now every moment more and more scorchingly in love with her, and

liked her as she was. It is true, however, that for
the time being, he could have wished her more
complaisant, for, so soon as he began to speak of
a slippery plan he had, her mood was still not to
listen. She would do nothing but walk the floor,
rail, and swear she'd have Colpoys on his knees
confessing how many mud-cats he'd befooled
her for; and the Chevalier, brushed out of the
way with "Futs" and "Poohs", felt keenly that
too much time might pass before she'd hear him.
He was not a man to shout her down or hold her
with his hand upon her mouth till she gave ear;
his desperation could never go so far, yet he was
desperate, as the plan he had in mind is proof.

Upon the calamitous accident to the Bishop,
Mrs. Jinny had suddenly become not only a treas-
ure in the heart of M. de Champvallon; with the
miscarriage of her assault upon the churchman,
her preservation was made, to the young Frenchman's view, a charge upon his honor. She had
conceived the jest for his entertainment and to
win astonishment from him, he knew; no more
rigid obligation could rest upon him than to see
that she did not suffer for it. To this end he could

spare neither himself nor any other, and, though
he knew the third of the jesting party to be of
like disposition, he looked to him for little aid.
Mr. Chedlowe, indeed, might be ruinous at any
time for lack of brains.

At the topmost of an outburst of Mrs. Jinny's, he drew the Chevalier into the bedchamber.
"You hear her?" he asked, as if hearing her could
have been avoided within the house. "I do believe
she's done with Colpoys at last! She takes her
oath on it over and over, and so I—"

"Hush! Hush!" de Champvallon said pity-
ingly. "Come into the big room with me and let
'er be alone. Walk loudly."

They went into the hall; M. de Champvallon
picked up his thin rapier and stepped noisily
about while he fastened its embroidered belt and
shoulder-scarf upon him. Mr. Chedlowe, taking
up his own sword, imitated the Chevalier's action,
and then both stood listening, through two doors
left open, to the sharp footsteps in the kitchen.
There was a crash as of crockery swept from a
table to the floor; then she came swishing
through the bedchamber and into the hall.

"What! What!" she cried. "You snake your-selves away from me?"

The Chevalier laughed aloud. "Ah, Jeeny! 'Ow many feet 'as a snake? We stamped with every step we took."

"Well, it brought me!" she said; but not meekly. "For what?"

"To say it in one word," he replied, "so that two frien's of yours—Misterr Chedlowe and me —shall not become too intimate with a gallows."

"Pooh!" she said. "What's this talk of hang-ing?"

"Ah, she ask' us!" M. de Champvallon clapped Mr. Chedlowe lightly upon the shoulder, as if in congratulation. "She ask' us the question; there-fore she will listen to the answer. When we spoke of danger to 'er, she would 'ear nothing; but now that we speak of ourself she listen'."

"I do not! I listen to none of your prattling! I've other—"

"Ah, but if we speak of Misterr Colpoys?" the Chevalier interrupted quickly. "If 'e is to be pun-ish' for you—"

"I'll let you speak of that," she said. She stood

by one of the cumbersome chairs, and suddenly she sat down, looking at the two young men before her. "What have you to say of that?"

"You are more like our French Henri le Grand than ever!" M. de Champvallon cried in brightest approval. "Excellent! After 'e would lose 'is sagacity during a passion 'e would alway' recover it—with the 'elp of 'is frien's."

Jinny's gilt-heeled shoe was tapping the floor. "Well? Well? Your highest praise of anything is always the same: that it is like something French. That's not the flattery to me you think it. Did you ask me to listen to—"

"To something that may please you more than stupid praise from a poor Frenchman," he said sadly. He closed the door of the bedchamber; then came to where she sat, with Chedlowe standing beside her, and in a low voice told them of his meeting with Mr. Brunnage and what talk he had with the Justice.

Mr. Chedlowe was puzzled by a point in the narrative. "What?" he asked. "What did yon Brunnage say Colpoys is become?"

"A Quecka."

"In heaven's name, what's that?"

Here, to his own regret, M. de Champvallon was somewhat vague. "I did not wish to ask too much. 'E tell me it is an infidel viper w'ich plot agains' the King and surely did make the great misfortune of our poor Bishopp because 'e preach' agains' the Quecka."

"Quaker!" Jinny cried, springing up. "By my bones, he means Tom's suspected to be a Quaker!"

"Yes. What is it—Quecka?"

"Quaker! Quaker!" Mr. Chedlowe explained impatiently. "A heathen sect that shakes and quakes afeared o' fighting."

Jinny turned upon him, laughing angrily. "Your mind's eye sees Tom doing that? Quaker! You're witless! What clown's head has your oaf Brunnage on his shoulders? Why, Tom Colpoys—" She interrupted herself with an outcry of inspiration. "Ah! The tricky dog! I've seen these Quakers; they garb all in sad color and so was when I catched him yonder a while ago! So was that fusty-haired drab with him a very drab, for she was drab from head to foot! She-

Quaker all over, no question, and now at last I know this villain Colpoys and what he's done! Made pretense to be a Quaker to win the she-Quaker! Ay, he's a Quaker—while he likes her!"

Again she outspokenly said more; but M. de Champvallon interposed persuasively. "Does it matter so much if 'e is truly one of these conspirators or if 'e naughtily preten' to be one for 'is love's sake? What put' 'im at your mercy is that Misterr Bron-age belief 'im to be truly one."

"At my mercy?" Jinny, pacing again, swept round to face the Chevalier, halting before him. "Who did ever have Tom Colpoys at mercy? When could I hope to have him there?"

"Now," M. de Champvallon said quietly. "At this moment."

"Don't fiddle to me!"

"I would if I could," he said, and bowed to her. "But I was never taught any skill in that art. Without music, then, I tell you that Misterr Bron-age is as sure in 'is soul as death that this busy lover of a Colpoys is a Quecka and so did make that troublesome slaughter of the Bishopp. Misterr Bron-age will meet the brother of the poor Bishopp, and, after they talk, both will think the same thing. I can even suspect they 'ave 'ad a meeting by this time and that they are thinking much about this 'ouse of Misterr Colpoys, where the poor Chedlowe and I mus' wait in patience for a lady to be our leader again."

"You say the truth!" Chedlowe cried. "We should 'a' been out o' here and away from Wanton Mally as soon as Jinny was come."

She laughed. "Was that why you was snoring, Rafe?"

"Sleep felled us all," the Chevalier reminded her. "There was no 'elp from it; sometime' it will 'ave its way. But I think that when we began to sleep it was already too late to go from Vanton Mallee, because by then all way' from it was watch'."

"Then we're closed in it now," Jinny said. "Is that what you tell me?"

"It is one thing I tell you."

"Then why make a pother about whether we're in this house or out of it?"

"Patience," he begged. "Only a little more. For victory in war we mus' alway' think with the

mind of the enemy. So what will be the thought
of Bron-age and the Colonel Bourne when they
meet? I am sure of this: they will say, 'Colpoys
is look' for at 'is 'ouse at dark; 'e will not go there
sooner, so that is what we mus' not do, too, or
risk the chance to frighten 'im away and make
ourself more difficulty to catch 'im.' So then, my
Jeeny, until the dark we are as safe 'ere as we
could be out of the 'ouse. It is as though we are
under a tree on an island; there is a storm and
while it rage' we cannot go away from the
island, and, until the wind become' strong
enough to blow the tree down, we are as safe
under it as some other place. Well, we think that
the wind is going to blow the tree down very
soon after the dark but not before."

"Not before, we *think?*" Chedlowe said.
"How long will you hold the lady in talk beneath your tree that may be ready to fall?"

"Be still!" Jinny bade him, and looked at the
Chevalier. "Come to it! What of this punishing
you offered me?"

"Well, what punishment do you English make
for these—these Quecka?"

She was contemptuous instantly. "For pretending to be one, nothing! For being one, gaol sometimes. Is that all?"

"No, but—" He put his right forefinger upon the side of his handsome nose and seemed to deal with a perplexity. "Well—I 'ad a thought. If Misterr Bron-age and the Colonel Bourne come in this 'ouse and discover only Misterr Colpoys and 'is dear lady and 'er kind 'usban', they would say, 'Ah! These are the three!' and take them away."

"Tush, yes, they might or they might not—as Quakers!" Jinny said. "Your Brunnage may be Quaker-mad; but they'd show him they'd no hand to the Bishop's hurt, and where'd we be? Why, out on your island of Wanton Mally with the storm on us!"

He seemed to regret his stupidity. "Ah, in a breath she blow' it all away! She remember' what I forget—that the picture she put into the mind of the pursuer is of a woman and two men and a white 'orse, a black 'orse and a bay 'orse. So if we ride away, the pursuer come' 'ere and discover' a woman and two men and a servant and three bay 'orses. Then these three people and the servant they say, 'We know nothing of a bishopp. On Vanton Mallee you will find a lady on a white 'orse and two gentlemen on a black and a bay.'" The Chevalier sank down upon a chair despondently. "It is a pity. I 'ave nothing more to say."

"Haven't you?" Jinny cried, for now she had in her mind what he had put there. "I have! Ah, Colpoys, Colpoys, now I'll talk to you for the last time!" She ran to a window and saw him standing outside, where he stared through the fog after Lecky; then she turned toward M. de Champvallon, who rose. "You stayed me when I'd have followed him a while ago; you'd best not stay me now."

"No," he said. "Dear child, go to 'im. You are wise again and we 'ave nothing but obedience." He opened the door, and bowed as she ran out by him; then he closed it and turned to Chedlowe. "Our Jeeny rescue' us, I think."

"Does she? Does she?" Mr. Chedlowe asked fretfully. "I do not know what she does or what you do, and I'd be better pleased with plainer speaking. What's she afoot?"

The young Frenchman's fine smile became sorrowful. "A lovers' las' meeting, I am afraid, my poor Chedlowe. For my part, I am a little console', for I am sure it will not be a tender one." Then he sighed and was earnest. "For all that, I would be willing to take 'is place. She is a lady the mos' debonnaire and passionate I 'ave ever the privilege to see and—yes, I think 'e is going to be in a great trouble; but I would take 'is place."

Mr. Chedlowe was irritated. "Plainer speaking, I said. Plainer speaking, Champvallon! What's she afoot?"

M. de Champvallon roused himself from a short but melancholy revery. "This, my frien': that she and you and I will ride away from 'ere on three bay 'orses, and leave our own for Mis· terr Colpoys and 'is pretty lady and 'er 'usban'."

"What! Why, how—" Chedlowe caught his breath sharply, withheld it, then exhaled audibly. "So! So! Why, 'twould do the trick, I'll swear! If Bourne and Brunnage find a white and a black and a bay horse here with those three that are already damned for Quakers—why, Lecky could take his oath to anything and they'd hold him a

liar for that he's Colpoys's servant, and they
could all four swear their hearts out that we'd
been here and taken their horses; but your Brunnage and the Colonel would think them striving
to wheedle justice with crazy tales, and so would
any court they're haled before. By my soul,
'twould do the trick!"

"I think it would," the Chevalier said, looking at him thoughtfully. "I am not English, but
you are and should know what your people will
do. Misterr Bron-age know' there is a Frenchman on a bay 'orse who is somewhere not very
far. What if the poor Colpoys say to Misterr
Bron-age, 'One of the three people in what you
think my crazy tale was a Frenchman on a bay
'orse.' Éh? What you say of that?"

"Why, Brunnage would only believe Colpoys
the greater liar. Brunnage would think Colpoys
had met you by chance on the moor, as he himself did, and that Colpoys trickily sought to add
you as substance to the thinness of his lie. Why,
man, man, to give Quakers to Bourne and Brunnage as destroyers of a bishop is to put into their
jaws the meat they pant for! How long do you

think Col'nel Bourne'll listen before he eats? Once he takes 'em he'll be on his way to London with 'em in a matter o' minutes, and those that watch the borders o' the moor'll be called in, so't we can ride from the moor ourselves without any to hinder. What's plainer?"

M. de Champvallon was still thoughtful. "Later there will be a trial, éh?"

"Not much later!" Rafe Chedlowe said, and laughed. "Have no misgivings; we'll not be drawn into it. With such a case against 'em, do you think they'll get much shrift or that they'll be listened to? Why, being Quakers, they'll not swear and so their testimony can't be used. Nor will any be used for 'em, Champvallon, because there'd be none to swear they saw 'em here or there at such and such a time, except another Quaker, who likewise wouldn't swear and so'd be unheard. If Colpoys pretends, as Jinny says, and if he would swear, why, a man of his old repute in London being now catched with Quakers, and such a case against him, I do think he'd be howled at from the very bench! No, no! When Bourne rides into London with these three he'd best have more troopers with him than he has now, else his prisoners'll be torn from him and the crowd'll have 'em. If we take their horses now, I tell you the rest o' the matter's as plain as day."

"It mus' be." The Chevalier looked at him with a wan satire, imperceptible to Mr. Chedlowe. "If it is so plain to you, it mus' be plain."

"Well," Chedlowe said, rubbing his chin. "You're a Frenchman and may not think as I do; but, to my mind, it's an ill thing to do. If she's not done with Colpoys, as you've showed me, and still pines for him, why, I hate him; yet it's an ill thing to do."

"I think so, my poor Chedlowe. Will you tell me something else we can do that will 'ave some certainty of bringing our Jeeny safe 'ome?"

"Something else? Why, no; there's no other way to make sure she'd be safe." Chedlowe glanced out of the window uneasily. "But what's she afoot with him now? Why does she talk with him? We should bring her in and tell her what we're to do."

"She know'."

"How does she? She didn't speak of it."

"My poor Chedlowe! She know', and that is why she wish' to speak with him a las' time."

"But why?" Chedlowe cried. "If she knows, why would she speak with him again?"

"I think I can tell you one reason," M. de Champvallon said. "It would be only one where there are many; but I think it is the stronges'. She is not like you and me. We do not love this Colpoys, since she does, and it would be our desire to destroy 'im honorably; but that is denied us. We are compel' to do it naughtily for 'er sake, and so we do it. But she is a woman and mus' 'ate 'im with a great fierceness or she cannot do it. So she talk' with 'im this las' time to be sure she 'ate 'im enough."

Mr. Chedlowe, at the window, grew more uneasy. "But if she find she do not? She might tell him what we think to do and—"

"My poor Chedlowe! With that other woman in the same 'ouse? And she as blonde as Jeeny but of a prettier face!"

CHAPTER X

OLPOYS heard Jinny coming behind him, glanced over his shoulder, and then with reluctance turned to face her. She saw the reluctance and breathed faster; but she had command of herself and came to a stop before him with her eyes cast down and her hands clasped behind her. "There was a fog the second time I came here," she said in a gentle voice. "You do not remember."

"I remember very well, Jinny."

"The third time I came there was only a gauzy mist after a rain, and the sun played in it, so that

147

the thatch of your house was all a saffron twinkle. I thought it very pretty—when I came. I
saw nothing pretty when I went away." Now
she smiled, but watched him slyly through her
lashes. "I think my leaving you was what let you
see prettiness again."

"Now, now," he protested. "You can't know
what I saw when you had gone."

Jinny laughed with an indulgence he recognized as perilous. "We'll not speak of that," she
said. "Already you look browbeat in that old
way of yours, and I'll not browbeat you again.
I'll not beat you with either my hands or my
words; I'll trouble you no more. I mean never.
You think I'm not earnest? You think I could
never free myself of the yearning to torment
you?"

"Oh, no—"

"Oh, yes," she said, gently mocking him. "You
couldn't believe this the end of my troubling
you, because you think the wizardry you put
upon me once is everlasting and so works in me
that all my life I must tease you to give me again
the sweetness I had from you and that you took

away from me. You think I can no more quit
my teasing than you can quit denying me. Ah,
I know you mightily wish it wasn't so! Well, I
do believe that's a wish you can have fulfilled;
but, for your good manners' sake, you mustn't
seem too gay with the news that I can rid you of
me."

"No," Colpoys said. "I'm not gay, Jinny."

"That's well; sadness may become you, for the
end of my teasing might be a pleasantry not to
your benefit—I'm still as wild a jester, Tom, as
once we both were, together. Well, I've a jest in
mind, and, when it's done and you feel the point
of it, you'll think of me and how I rid myself of
my slavery to the teasing of you. Then, it may
be, you'll remember all that's passed between us
—how you found me young and eager and was
my merry teacher, and, when you'd fashioned
me to be another very self for you, why, then
behold! I was tedious for you and so you was
gone into fasting and meditation for the saving
of your soul! My own soul could shift for itself, éh, Tom?"

What she said stirred an old trouble within

him, as his face showed. "I did you no good. When I came first to Wanton Mally my thought of you was that I'd better you by my absence."

"Yes? And by your silence, too?"

"On my honor, I thought so, Jinny. Then when you came here you'd listen to nothing but my going back to the town with you. You—"

"Oh, yes," she said quietly. "I was the very wickedness you fled from. Wanton Mally kept you holy and I must begone from it without you."

"Jinny! Jinny!" he said desperately. "What did you bring here but your anger? Did you listen?"

"Yes," she answered, trembling. "To lies!"

"No, not to one. The little listening you did was to what couldn't find you. You say I let your soul shift for itself; but you never showed me your soul."

"Because I have none to show?"

"None you was willing to show to me, Jinny. When you came here you would speak of nothing but that I should go back with you. I must give you that one proof I loved you better than my soul—I must give you that or nothing! Was it so?"

"Why was it so?" she asked with sudden heat, and spoke rapidly. "When you leave a woman for your soul's sake, will she ask less? Ah, and when you leave her as you did me, like orange-peel by your seat when you'd gone from the playhouse! Oh, your soul, your soul, Master Col-poys! You made me a mortal jealousy of your soul and then wished me to content myself with my own as you did with yours. You think I didn't know all you'd have said to me? Why should I have listened when I knew? Do you think I'd never heard before of all those old hy-pocrisies and cantings? You made me think o' my grandmother!"

"Well," he said, "I think she might be thought of without hurt to you, Jinny." There was a mel-ancholy twinkle in his eyes, as he spoke; but no responding glint from hers, which were like his in being hazel, yet unlike in never twinkling.

"I hated her," she said. "I hate her again when she speaks from you; I'm an instance of what's modern and I have as much belief in her old pre-

tenses as I have in your new ones. Now, for the
last time, I'll tell you the true reason why I'd not
listen to you when you talked with her tongue:
I never believed you!"

"Your unbelief's not shrewd, Jinny."

"What!" she cried. "Why, here we stand, you
saying I'm a fool for never believing you, and I
rejoicing that I was not the fool you'd have had
me! Not shrewd, eh? You lived for four things
and loved 'em: wine, dice, fighting and me—me
most of all, when I first took the place of the
sweetheart that went before me, and then not at
all when another took mine and you loved her,
in turn, most of all."

"No. No other—"

"Fut!" she said. "You'll not forsooth me! I
knew it was another or more than one other.
When a man lives for four things he loves, and
hides away, forgetting three of 'em, it's for the
fourth, and that, with you, is a woman. Lord! to
think you hoped to cozen me into believing you
alone on Patmos with holy visions! You think I
knew so little what manner of man you are? You
can persuade me you could live in meditation?

Why, you're a man that's restless; you must ever be doing, doing—you can't live except with action. Not shrewd, éh? I knew this much, I tell you; if you stayed on Wanton Mally, and you did, it was because you found enough to do here! Well, do you answer?"

"Jinny! Jinny!" he said in despair. "I have nought to do with any of the four things you say I loved."

"What!" she cried. "When at last I've seen what you do here!"

"You have not seen what I do here."

"So! So!" she said triumphantly, and laughed. "Now we come to it! At last you tell me there are doings here. Wanton Mally's not all for meditation, then, you sad-colored saint? After three years I begin to get the truth from you, that you're here less for thinking than for doing!"

"Jinny," he said, "I would have told you what I do here; but you had such a rage at me I couldn't hope you'd keep the matter private."

"No?" She made her face blank; then smiled brightly at him and put her hands before her, open toward him, as if to show how quiet she was, and how frank. "You see I'm in no rage now. I wish my ring had not hurt your lip; that was a little gust of rudeness without time for judgment, and if you'd stayed I'd have asked your forgiveness quickly. So tell me what you've done and do on Wanton Mally."

"I think I must," he said. "You have not seen what I do here; but you've seen something, and I fear you might speak of it when you ride on, and so bring harm on me and on my betters, too."

She shook her head gently. "No; don't mar it, Tom. Tell me the truth as if for no better reason than my asking it of you. You speak of harm to your—to your betters. You mean the she-Quaker you have with you?"

"I thought it," he said, pondering. "I thought you might guess she is a Quaker. That's what you mustn't speak of, Jinny—that you saw Quakers here."

"No? Nor of the feigned Quaker with 'em?"

"Feigned Quaker? Who's that?"

"Excellent!" she said, and seemed to rally him in high good-nature. "You're changed not a whit,

Tom; you're the same merry droll. Kynaston himself was never cunninger at putting upon his face that look of innocence and puzzling. 'Who's that?' quoth he, as if feigning to be a Quaker lay beyond his understanding!"

Colpoys was enlightened; but only to the increase of the plaintive in his voice. "I? I'm not a Quaker nor feigning anything. I'd be one if I could."

"No doubt, old lad, no doubt!" she laughed. "Well, if you'd be one, why aren't you?"

"I think because," he cried, "I'm not yet kind enough."

"Oh! Oh!" Jinny cried, showing him mock frowns and chiding gestures. "Not kind enough to she-Quakers, you stony villain?"

"Not kind enough and not meek enough," he said, ignoring her merriment. "I think the world lives in a false wisdom, Jinny, because it needs a false wisdom to give it the bravado to live for itself. It grows in body-pleasures, and that's to be spendthrift of the spirit; it grows in ambitious pride, and that's to be cruel."

"Grandmother! Dear grandmother!"

"So be it," he said mildly. "Self-righteousness, too, grows in the world; I must keep from that. But I've seen these sober folk, the Friends, walking their own way in a world that cudgeled 'em for it, yet couldn't gain their resentment, and so, to my thinking, they were above the world."

"Above the rest of us, to your thinking?"

"Above me," he said, now as wistfully earnest as she was seemingly light. "Meekness is a part of their kindness, and I've striven hard to find that meekness in me; but it doesn't come. Times I think it's nigh me and that I could bear blows and stand quiet—and then I know I couldn't." He sighed heavily. "If ever I could be struck and give a gentle answer—"

She glinted the diamond upon her finger close to his eyes. "Shall I try your lip with that again?"

"Oh, from you—"

"Useless, I see," she said. "From me or any woman it would be no test and you could not be sure whether or no you're fit for a Quaker. I see! Then there's a kindness could be granted you —to get you struck by a gentleman so that you could put yourself to the proof and discover if you're true or feigned as a Quaker. I'll think of this on your behalf, Tom; but first you was to tell me what you do with Quakers on Wanton Mally."

"Jinny, will you pledge me your honor you'll not speak of it?"

"I will," she said, with a smile that was a riddle. "I'll tell none, on my very honor."

"Well, I do what my ability lets me to help these kind poor folk. Many that I learned were to have writs against them I've fetched here and led on a little way to a ship I have that carries them to plantations granted me in the provinces across the sea. That's all the truth, Jinny."

She shook her head gayly. "Oh, no! That's something of what you've done, perhaps. I'm curious and ask to know what you do. I mean the pretty lady that's here now—with her husband."

"Why, no more than that," he said. "I'm carrying them to the ship, Jinny, as I carried the others."

"How soon?"

"Why—very soon."

She nodded as if satisfied; then seemed to have a second thought. "How long has she been with you—she and her husband?"

"Not all of two days."

"So quickly!" she said musingly. "But they were known to you before, I'm sure."

"Not long."

"No? Well, I was not long, myself! What was it? Was it an hour or only the half of one before you saw the looks I couldn't hide? Or perhaps you don't remember, or, if you do, perhaps you've seen others so much readier to be daft that the time I took to it seems long? This she-Quaker, for an instance."

"You cling tight to your misunderstandings," he said. "Anne Tanner dearly loves her husband."

"I'm sure she does! So would I, most dearly, if I had one and if I desired to show another gentleman how dear a husband he cost me."

In desperation Colpoys turned from her; then wheeled back to face her, and suddenly put a hand upon her shoulder and laughed, all friendly.

"Why, Jinny, it's as if you irked yourself to be angrier and angrier with me for the sake of a desire to hate me. In my life I've liked no other so well, either man or woman. There's a rashness in you that could be lofty; but when I was with you I turned you only to folly. Well, I think I blundered in my manner of leaving you, because any manner of leaving you went so hard with me that I thought the shortest and most vacant held the least anguish. That's all you can find to hate in me, and hate it if you will but don't pant to feed the hatred—not even if I'm your grandmother again and tell you that feeding hatred's rubbing a sore to be sorer, and kindness is the only thing in the world that's grateful for feeding; it spouts honey back at you if you give it a drop. Come, Jinny dear, be kinder!"

She looked at him hatefully and began to speak with fierceness. "Oh, my grandmoth—" she said. But all at once she trembled, not with anger, and her lip twitched pathetically. "Why did you misuse me?" she asked. "I mean when I'd have kept her in the room to answer me and excuse herself for being here. Why did you bruise my wrist and lift me and bear me across the room and thrust me towards the wall for her sake?"

M. le Chevalier de Champvallon, watching from a window and seeing Colpoys with his hand still upon Jinny's shoulder, was aware, too, even through the mist, of the expression with which her eyes searched his host's face when she asked this question. M. de Champvallon was suddenly filled with alarm.

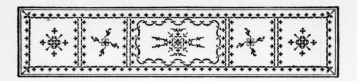

CHAPTER XI

T HE noble young French traveller, abreast of the best attitude in his own country, would have said of himself that in all his relations to life he was a philosopher. He could be readily a duellist, or, without hesitation, could put his fortune upon the hazard of a gaming table or his life upon the chance that a lady's window could be opened soundlessly; but, however vitally any such matter engaged him, his pride was to maintain in mind, as well as in manner, the posture of a man who deals with what is sympathetically amusing but inconsequent. The

161

truth of him is that like many another of his fellow-countrymen he was, in the operation of his life and of his thoughts, not a philosopher but an artist. It was the artist's heart within him that had been stirred by Jinny Wilmot; he saw her as the most vivid portrait in a gallery of ladies and had a great desire to add some touches to the canvas, himself. He loved to put Jinny's face through a variety of aspects: to make it smile and to make it laugh; to make it brood, then grow impatient, then rage. Thus, under grim pressure at Mally Older, and for her sake, he was still an artist and still painted what expressions he chose upon her face; but now he feared his brush had slipped. It was far from his intention that she should look tenderly at Colpoys.

He turned from the window, muttered to Chedlowe that he would "take the air" for a time, and went to a door opposite that of the bedchamber known to him. The latch yielded; he went into a second bedchamber, thence through two others and so into a little room cluttered with books of a dreary appearance; but here he found what he sought, a door that let

him out, with the length of the house and its out-
buildings between him and any roving glance of
Jinny Wilmot's. He walked lightly to the rear of
the stables, entered and found the tanner and his
pretty wife rearranging a saddle-pack. The
Chevalier looked politely disappointed.

"No?" he said. " 'E is not with you? Misterr
Colpoys?"

Francis was on his knees before the pack; but
jumped up. "I'll fetch him."

"No." The Chevalier detained him quickly
with the word. "You are a man w'ich love' a
'orse, so I wish you and Misterr Colpoys together
will look at mine and think if I should give 'im
some medicine."

"That bay beside the black? Why, he's as
stout as—"

"No, no," M. de Champvallon said with hurried solicitude. " 'E cough. Now 'e stand still, 'e
do not; but all the morning while 'e is ridden, 'e
cough. Please come put your 'and upon 'im with
me and if we could ask Misterr Colpoys—" He
looked at Anne, as if absently.

She rose cheerfully from beside the pack and

went to the open doorway opposite to that just
entered by the Chevalier. "A little while ago he
was near by with friend Lecky," she said. "I'll
tell him he's needed." She went out briskly and
saw Colpoys with Jinny before the main part of
the house; moreover, she saw that Jinny instantly
saw her and changed a posture that had a kind of
humbleness in it for one that was all rigidity.

Colpoys's back was toward the Quakeress; but
he turned to see what brought the change upon
Jinny. Anne came something more than half
way, hesitated, then stopped. Her color was high
but her heart was not; she and Francis had been
mobbed at Biddesley and then she was not afraid,
yet now at Mally Older she feared the great London dame she'd called a "perisher for pleasure".

"Well, Anne?" Colpoys said encouragingly.

"When she's said her say," Anne began, and
felt that it was a poor beginning, vulnerable to
misinterpretation. "When the dame's finished
with thee——" She stopped and tried again.
"When thou'st heard all her say——"

This time she was stopped by Jinny's laughter,
which was noisy. "Why, here's kindness! Your

she-Quaker's restless when you're a little with
me, yet grants me the time to have my say out,
so that she stands by to listen until she fetches
you away! Didn't I say I thought she might be
as quick with you as others have been, Tom? Go
with her; go with her, old lad, for I'll not keep
you!"

"Nay," Anne said. "I'll wait. I mean the matter'll wait. I—" But with Jinny's laughter noisier
upon this, she could say no more. Breathless, she
turned and went back to the stables, having done
much better for M. de Champvallon than he had
hoped. His thought had been that the mere sight
of her would be enough to freshen what he
wished to be refreshed within Jinny, and his
thought was shrewd—Anne Tanner was never
lovelier than when she blushed, as he was sure she
would—but she had done more than let herself
be seen blushing.

Jinny's laughing stopped sharply and she stared
after the Quakeress with what seemed a placid
thoughtfulness. "I didn't know they went bare-
head so often, these Quakers," she said. "I
thought they—but no, if they have hair like

that!—and a face so cunningly aware of its own harmony, with little features in such pleased agreement with one another—No, no! She-Quakers'd never cover such hair or shade skin so pink and white with the modest headgear I've heard they boast of. She's been uncovered all her time with you, hasn't she, Tom?"

He moved his arm as if to place his hand where it had been when she dislodged it at the sight of Anne; but Jinny jerked back her shoulders and prevented him. "You hate me again so soon, Jinny?"

"Well, don't you give me cause?" Then, for that last moment—he had asked the question with a wistfulness that shook her—Jinny's mood again wavered; but Colpoys had no art like M. de Champvallon's, and least of all did he possess the Chevalier's understanding of Jinny.

"How do I give you cause now?" he asked.

"What! When you bruise me for her, thrust me to the wall for her, throw bolts against me to go with her, and, when you dare to stand alone with me for the twinkling of an eye, you turn

away from me because you've made her so calf-
sick for you she comes running—"

"Turn away from you? Yes, to ask her what
she wished, so she'd go," he said, and was so far
wise, for Jinny was a little pleased; but then, as
he was a frank, outspoken man by nature, he
thought to settle Jinny's doubts completely, and
he did. "Hark to you," he said, and laughed in a
way that begged her for an open good-fellow-
ship with him. "I have the task to put this tanner and his wife where they'll not be harmed for
their goodness; that's all. They're two pretty
hearts, gentle but would keep their faith in a
gaol with the plague in it, and I mustn't fail 'em.
Come, you'll not wish me to fail 'em, I'm certain! Why, Jinny, this Anne is a sweet, kind
woman; I'll tell you what she thinks o' me: she
has thanks for me, and that's natural for the
service I do her and her husband; but beyond
these thanks all that she feels is the wish I'd become a true Quaker. There's a 'light' she'd be
glad to bring me, she's said often; she thinks it
will come to me—and truly I hope it will. Now
what's there in this to make a pother? Why, she

and her husband both pray constantly that this
'light' may come upon me for my soul's sake,
she told me, and said her life would be little cost
to pay to bring it to some soul. Why, Jinny, her
whole thought o' me is for my soul."

"Sweet!" Jinny said in a dead voice. "Sweet!
Sweet! Sweet! So, I think already she has two
soul-husbands."

"Why, what?" he cried, startled more by her
look than by what she said. "Why, I've told
you—"

"So you have," Jinny said, nodding. "You've
told me, and now I have the whole of it at my
fingers' ends. Take heart, old lad; she'll bring you
the 'light', the 'light' your poor soul needs. Before it comes, though, I must cry quits with you.
I mean what I spoke of when I promised to rid
you of me."

"Ah, Jinny, you're angry with me again,
truly!"

"Why, yes!" she cried, her voice grown astrin-
gent. "Truly, I think I'm angry truly—as I need
be, I tell you, Colpoys—as I need be if I'm
to rid you of me. How am I to rid myself of this

trouble in me that makes me come teasing you?
Why, here's the answer: I've been tedious for
you, I've been a worry to your poor soul, I've
fretted you; but, with all this and all that, never
brought true harm to you, never did you a brave
hard hurt. How if that's what's needed for your
riddance of me and my riddance of my trouble
that's so wearying for us both?"

He saw and heard her dreadful earnestness,
and was alarmed. "To do me a hurt? What will
you do, Jinny?"

"Why, how if I set in motion that pleasantry
I spoke of? Oh, a singular good jest."

"What jest?" he asked, his anxiety sharply increased. "Jinny, you'll not forget my honor's
concern to keep these two poor Friends in safety?
You'll not betray—"

"Not a word of their being Quakers, Colpoys,
I swear; not a word o' that!"

"But if you harm me now, there's no help for
it but to harm them with me. Jinny, what's in
your mind to do?"

"Ho, Colpoys, begging?" She shook her head,
giving him looks from wild and dangerous eyes.

"Don't you know all pleasantries are spoiled when they're told to the butt of them afore they're loosed?"

He caught at her hands, uselessly; she walked backward from him as he followed. "I must know what's in your mind—I must know!"

She put her hands behind her and halted, puckering her brow. "Well, let me think. If you must know, I'll think of something to tell you; so you'll be easy. My fancy's not barren." She cleared her forehead and smiled at him. "Oh, here's a brave thought; I'm glad it comes to me! How if I do you that service your soul needs most, so that you can discover whether or not you're worthy of her? Why, yes, I'll do this for you, Tom. If I have you beat by a gentleman and you stand craven, you'll know you're her own true Quaker, and so shall I!"

"What, Jinny? You—"

"Ho, excellent!" She clapped her hands, applauding herself. "If you tremble with rage and fight, why, that's failure for you, and she'll weep; but if you quake under cuffing like a true Quaker it'll show all three of us, you and her

and me, that your soul's saved at last and she's
brought you the 'light'! So then, if that's proved
and you're shown to be her Quaker surely, I'll
heap pleasantry on pleasantry and let you see that
other merry jest I have in mind."

"Will you listen?" he said. "I've put a charge
upon myself to carry this poor man and his wife
to the ship. Until that's done I'll risk no hurt to
myself for any cause—last of all for a sour
whimsy of yours."

"Whimsy? Whimsy?" She laughed with shrill-
ness and stepped toward the house.

"So that's why Rafe Chedlowe's with you,"
Colpoys said bitterly. "And the Frenchman, too,
if Rafe fails!"

But at this she turned back at him in open
fury. "I did not! Ah, now I'll do it for your
never having one thought of me that isn't hateful. Those two are with me for no reason that has
to do with you; but, since you think they have,
they shall have! No rest for me now, Colpoys,
until I'm quits with you!"

She turned again and ran into the house. He
turned, too, almost as quickly, but in the direc-

tion of the stables, and went that way in haste. M. de Champvallon had decided for himself that no medicine would be needed for his horse and had returned apologetically to the hall; Master Tanner and his wife were busy with another of their packs when Colpoys strode through the doorway. He unbuckled his belt, removed his sword from him and hung it upon a peg in a rough cupboard near the door.

Anne, on her knees, watched his face as he did this; then, as he turned from the cupboard to go out again, she sprang up, blushing, and uttered a little cry of happiness. "Oh, thou'lt leave it here behind thee forever? The light's come, friend?"

He shook his head. "I'm not so good," he said. "I only leave it here until we go from Mally Older to-night. It's a clouterly thing to be ever whacking about a man's heels."

CHAPTER XII

MRS. JINNY clanged behind her the
outer door of the hall and stepped
fiercely toward two bowing gentlemen. "Now
which of you'll be first to fight Tom Colpoys for
a lady who's had put upon her what can't be
borne?"

"I will!" said Mr. Chedlowe, upon the instant.
"I'd sooner fight him than chouse him with the
horses."

"One moment!" the Chevalier interposed
quickly. "Jeeny, you desire to leave 'im and 'is

lady—and the 'usban'—to Misterr Bron-age and the Colonel Bourne?"

"I do!"

"Then we devote ourself to that. Ha! Misterr Chedlowe and I, we also 'ave thought of the 'orses, you see! Now we 'ave not very much time and—"

"I'll do nothing," Jinny said. "An you don't first make him fight, I'll do nothing!"

Through a window, M. de Champvallon peered upward at the sky, slightly hunched up his left shoulder, smiled and said, "I think there may be time; but, if there is or if there is not, you are a lady who mus' be satisfy. I will speak with Misterr Colpoys."

"You'll not!" Chedlowe cried, and stepped toward him. "You're too quick to think she looks to you, Frenchman!"

His manner was outrageously overbearing; M. de Champvallon gave him a glance and turned to Jinny with humorous appeal. "Two?" he asked. "Two duel' for me—the firs' one with Misterr Chedlowe? If you 'ave no desire for two, I think you mus' 'ush 'im."

"Rafe!" Jinny said. "Hold your gabble! Champvallon, I'll go with you; he's in the stables with his Quakers."

"No, dear child." The Chevalier pushed a chair back to the wall as he spoke, studied the light from the windows calculatingly, scuffed the floor to test its roughness and that of the soles of his shoes. "No; we mus' bring 'im 'ere and those others with 'im. You understan' me?"

"I do not. The sooner it's done—"

"Again a little patience! Let us put ourself to no trouble better to avoid. If nobody is in the stable' when we go there to leave this place, well, that make' it a little easier for us, you see. So, if we bring those people 'ere and I 'ave the good fortune to put Misterr Colpoys upon this floor, they will be busy with 'im 'ere for a time; we can pass to the stable' and go away without a word from a soul."

Jinny was scornful. "What! With Colpoys down, you make a pother lest you be stopped by Lecky and the she-Quaker's husband?"

"Your pardon," M. de Champvallon said, in apology for making his real thought in the matter clearer. "I think I shall be fortunate with Misterr Colpoys; but a such thing is never among the certainties of this life. If we are near the stable' and it is I and not 'e who shall be stretch upon the groun', I think 'e would so prove 'imself something of a master in the art and might be too strong for Misterr Chedlowe; you could not do by force what you wish. But if something 'appen' to me from Misterr Colpoys not so close to the stable', I promise to live long enough to make a such confusion that you and the good Chedlowe can slip to the stable' and be away in the fog upon two bay 'orses before Misterr Colpoys stop' you. So, you see, it is better to be done 'ere, my Jeeny."

"Fut!" she said. "He's not yet made to fight."

"Made to? Made to?" Mr. Chedlowe was astonished. "Why, where's your wits, Jinny? Wasn't you asking me if my mind's eye could see Colpoys afeared o' fighting? In the town was there any quicker to be titched into it?"

"Yes, in the town," she said, and looked at the Chevalier. "I'm still waiting to see what he'll do in Wanton Mally!"

"You 'ave wait' only while I explain to you why it should be 'ere," he said. "You shall wait longer only until I can bring 'im 'ere with 'is Quecka." M. de Champvallon permitted himself to put an element of dramatic reproach into the ceremonious bow he made to her before quitting the room. He went through the bedchamber, the kitchen and the passage, the door of which was unbolted, as he had thoughtfully returned by that way from his recent diplomatic errand; then, entering the stables with a casual air, he smiled benevolently upon the two Friends but addressed himself to their protector, who was at an outer door, departing. "If you please, Misterr Colpoys?"

Colpoys turned back. "Yes?"

The Chevalier cast an inquiring glance about the place; then said, "I beg for your pardon; but I am on an errand w'ich will excuse me, I think, if I seem to push myself into a matter not mine. I do not see your servant 'ere."

"Lecky? No, he's down the road."

"Ah? Then you three and ourself are all w'ich are near this place?"

"All I know of now," Colpoys informed him, somewhat surprised. "What's to do?"

"A little matter but not of unimportance to us all. Will you and this lady and 'er 'usban' come with me to the great room, if you please?"

"To the hall?" Colpoys was reluctant. "Why?"

"Sir," M. de Champvallon said, with formal gravity, "it is a lady's desire."

The information did not greatly reassure his host. "Jinny's?" he said. "Well, I don't—"

"Sir," M. de Champvallon repeated, with a deepened gravity, "it is a lady's desire."

"Oh, I'll come," Colpoys said. "What does she—"

"I will 'ave the honor to tell you when we are with 'er." M. de Champvallon went to the passage door and spoke to Francis. "Bring Madame."

"Me?" Anne asked, and took her husband's hand but looked uneasily to Colpoys. "What will she—"

Colpoys shook his head. "Who can say what she intends or desires? But it'll be best for us to know, Anne. Come, you and Francis."

Thus the four went through the passage and

to the bedchamber doorway that opened upon
the hall. M. de Champvallon had let the others
precede him; but at the door he went forward,
with Colpoys following, while the tanner and
his wife remained in the doorway. Jinny stared
at these two and laughed. "So that sparrow's the
husband!" she said. "I thought it would be so."

"You have business with us?" Colpoys asked
her. "Pray come to it as soon as may be."

"I? No." She waved a hand toward M. de
Champvallon, and, taking Chedlowe by the
sleeve, moved with him backward to the wall.
"Keep your sparrows in the door, Tom, if you'd
have 'em out of harm's way and not spoil sport.
I'll speak to you through the gentleman that
takes my cause upon him, Monsieur le Chevalier
de Champvallon."

"But he told me—" Colpoys began uneasily.

M. de Champvallon was already close to him
and touched him delicately upon the chin with
the back of a slim forefinger. "Misterr Colpoys, that is my stroke upon your face in revenge
for the manner in w'ich you receive' me when I
summon' you to speak with a lady. This is my

quarrel with you: you make objection'; you did
not come upon the instant but force' me to ask
you twice. Now you 'ave my stroke upon your
face and I am waiting."

"You'll not wait long!" Colpoys said harshly,
and, as hot color rushed in his cheeks, swung
about toward the door to the bedchamber. But
at the doorway two white faces confronted him.
Neither the little tanner nor his wife stepped
aside to make way for him and neither spoke to
him; but both looked at him in a tremulous sus-
pense. He stood still before them for a moment,
shook his head, smiled wryly and said, "No, I'll
not fetch it from the cupboard; but we'll leave
these folk."

"Pardon," M. de Champvallon said, and interposed himself between Colpoys and the two
Friends. "If you 'ave mislay your sword and 'ave
no other, I will borrow Misterr Chedlowe's for
you."

Colpoys turned his back upon him and took a
step toward the outer door, whereupon Chedlowe strode to oppose his passage, and Jinny
laughed and put herself before the door of the

bedchamber across the hall. The owner of Mally Older, grown pale, glanced at her with musing comprehension; then walked to the settle nearer him, before the fire, and sat down.

M. de Champvallon was not a foot behind him and tapped him several times upon the shoulder as he sat. "Sir, these are other strokes of mine upon your body. Your be'avior is not pretty; I mus' warn you it is so singular that if you 'ave no better answer for me I mus' brush the tip' of my finger' where they 'ave touch' you. What?" Then, as Colpoys neither spoke to him nor so much as glanced at him, but sat looking steadily at the other settle, in what strangely seemed a revery, the young Frenchman brought forth a kerchief of lace and with it fulfilled his threat. "You see?" He addressed himself to Jinny and Mr. Chedlowe. "As I 'ave no serving people with me to deal properly with this Colpoys, I am not able to do more in the matter."

"Oh, aren't you?" Jinny said, as pale now as Colpoys himself. "I asked you to make him fight! Will you do it?"

"I?" M. de Champvallon was surprised and reproachful. "Dear child, but you 'ave seen! For us 'e 'as no more existence. Now let us go."

"Go?" Jinny said, and turned to Chedlowe. "Have you better for me than this French frippery, Rafe?"

"That I have!" he answered, breathing hard.

"Then on him, boy!"

Chedlowe strode to the settle and stood before the seated figure there. "What's gone with your quick stomach for fighting, Colpoys?" he asked. "I'm a man that does what Jinny'd have done, and I hated you because she liked you, and now I hate you because she hates you. Here's to fetch your stomach back into you!" With his open right hand he struck Colpoys hard on the cheek, and Colpoys, though his head joggled with the blow, did not even look at him or change expression, but sat staring straight forward as if unmoved from his revery. "Why, what, no stomach yet?" Chedlowe bellowed at him, and slapped him again, with greater force. "Colpoys, Colpoys! Take these as favors from me to bring your stomach where it was!"

Again he struck and with a clinched hand,

twice, and a shrill outcry on indrawn breath came from Jinny with each blow. The swinging fist twice more marked Colpoys's face and swept back to strike again, but paused; for Francis and Anne Tanner came from the doorway, and Anne was within its range. "Off, you sparrows!" Chedlowe shouted at them, and laughed, pleased to use Jinny's word. "What? Will you fight me for him, sparrows?"

"Nay," Anne said breathlessly. "But if thou'lt strike us for him, we'll thank thee." She sat down beside Colpoys, upon his left, and took his left hand, while her husband passed to his right, sat and took his right hand.

"Let us be with thee, friend," the little tanner said humbly. "It is a great thing for Anne and me to be with thee in this hour. Thou'lt not deny us?"

"Nay," Colpoys said, "I'll not deny you, friends."

Anne was no longer afraid of the fierce London dame; now that the violence offered was bodily, she feared nobody, and in her look there was what held such violence to be as vulgar as it was futile. This eloquent look was a goad too stinging for Jinny; she swore at Chedlowe and rushed upon the settle.

"Pad-fist!" she cried. "You butter him to make him fight?" Chedlowe struck harder, and Jinny laughed uproariously; she thrust a mocking fore-finger against Colpoys's breast. "Fie, fie on a silly sight! Did ever mortal think to see this old em-broiler sit simpering 'twixt sparrows—sparrows that nurse his frighted hands! Why, Tom Col-poys, it shames me more for you to see you silly than to see you craven! Which have you the most of, Tom, fright or silliness? Oh Lord, to see the sight you are!" Her laughter stopped; she spoke hoarsely. "Oh, now I'll try you with what none that's a man can bear! I'll do the thing; but Rafe's my champion for you to avenge it on. See this!" With a ringed hand, she struck Anne upon the mouth as she had struck Colpoys, and cried: "How bully-boy? Will you fight for your woman?"

Colpoys did not look at her or speak, nor did Anne so much as touch a bruised lip; the three

The three sat in unchanged attitudes.

"He'll not so much as lift his hands to spare his head!"

sat in unchanged attitudes, and this was unbearable for Jinny Wilmot.

"Have you done what I bade you?" she shouted at Chedlowe. "Have you made him fight? Beat him! Beat him! Beat them all!" Beside herself, she did what she commanded Chedlowe to do, cuffed the three faces before her again and again with her full strength, and then, in a sobbing fury, turned with outstretched despairing arms to de Champvallon. "He'll not so much as lift his hands to spare his head!" she said. "He's so rotten with love of her, he does it to make her think she's saved his soul and's her true Quaker! Oh, the rogue, the rotten rogue!"

The Chevalier took her hands. "Come," he said with compassion. "You 'ave no more to do 'ere. It's enough, even for you."

He led her toward the bedchamber door. She looked back once, over her shoulder, at the discolored face of Colpoys, who sat motionless between two as still as he; then Jinny and M. de Champvallon and Chedlowe went out by that way and through the passage to the stables. There, Jinny stood in the outer doorway, shaking, her face to the fog, while the two gentlemen saddled three bay horses.

No sound could be heard from the house, no face was seen at a window, as the woman and two men rode forth again into Wanton Mally, nor were they themselves anything but silent; they had not said a word since they left the hall.

CHAPTER XIII

BLUFF-SPOKEN men will hush their voices in a fog as if some ominous presence might be listening: the hushing of the fog was all about Mally Older and came, too, into the hall, where the windows grew more opaque. The Chevalier de Champvallon, himself silent, was all too conscious of the silence from which he rode away; but a keener haunting went with him. Held in his mind's eye was what the fog looked in upon through those windows, and, in spite of every effort to be practical, he could not put that picture from him. Moreover, as he rode beside Jinny Wilmot, he knew that in the downbent blonde head under her great sherry-colored hat was the same vision and that she saw always before her, as he did, three still figures upon a settle in a darkening room. More, the Chevalier (for he felt it) knew what put sting into the heart of the beholder was the fact that the three figures sat unresentful; their bruised and cut faces showed only patience and their eyes had no rancor but seemed to dwell with a sad absence upon something afar. Thus those three had sat when the blows fell hard upon them, motionless except for the joggling of their struck heads—a joggling that might make a man sick if he could not rid himself of the memory of it—and the Chevalier was troubled by the fear that he was not to forget it. He had the same fear for Jinny, and, if he was to recover for himself something like an honorable part in an adventure now tinged with dishonor, he must at least take good care of her. Of this obligation, the present pressure was to bring her thoughts to matters more remediable than what had been done at Mally Older.

They were riding slowly in the direction of the King's Highway at the end of the Mally and had gone some hundreds of yards when he spoke. "You will laugh at me again for my admiration of our old Henri le Grand," he said. "But that was a very honest and gallant king, as I can prove, and I am very honest and gallant myself to praise 'im, for 'e possess' a grandson w'ich 'as put me to great inconvenience. Well, we mus' think like this, we mus' say to ourself, 'If Henri le Grand could be 'ere with us, what would 'e tell us to do?' You mus' leave this to me to answer, because an ancestor of mine was in love with that poor king's wife, Madame Marguerite, so I ought to know what Henri would tell us. I am sure 'e would say, 'Do not go too far, do not stay too near, and, although the road is a road nobody can see, keep away from it. '"

Mr. Chedlowe first grunted his scorn, then made it more elaborate. "Does it need one of your French kings to tell us that? Tom Fool'd be as wise!"

"Per'aps, per'aps," the Chevalier said, remaining urbane. "King Henri 'ad no English fog to 'elp 'im, so 'e mus' alway' use 'is brain. Well, let us use your fog and a little brain, too, per'aps.''

"Oh, fuddle-de-diddle!" Thus Mr. Chedlowe expressed an irritation engendered within him at Mally Older; for he, too, had an inner perception that something had gone wrong there, and the effect upon him was a vague yet distressful annoyance. He felt acutely the need to fight somebody. "Fuddle-de-diddle and folderoldol!"

The Chevalier gave him a glance but continued to address as much of the profile under the sherry-colored hat as he could see. "By this time I think Misterr Bron-age and those dragoon' will not be so far away from the 'ouse we 'ave lef'; but they will come from the other side from us. When they come a little near to the 'ouse, they will make a circle round it, not a very large one, because there are not enough of them. I am sure we are already beyond where that circle will reach, so we shall go a little farther and stop. If we go too far we might come to where people watch to see that nobody shall leave this Vanton Mallee, and there might be some questioning for us. I think we should choose some place not far away and res' there until after it is dark for two or three hour'; then I shall go back on my feet for a reconnaissance of the 'ouse, and, if the Colonel and those dragoon' are gone, we shall know that our way is clear for us and with a little care we can go on to the King's 'Ighway, sleep at an inn to-night and be on the road to London to-morrow. You agree with this?"

Jinny made no answer, for where there is no mind to listen, a sound is something lost in the ear. She fumbled under her skirt, not seeming aware that she did so, drew forth a thin little pouch of black silk and dropped it upon the ground, where it clinked faintly with the impact. The Chevalier was off his horse in an instant and had the pouch in his hand when Chedlowe, drawing rein and leaning down, snatched it from him mockingly.

"What, what! Money-mad, are you, Champvallon? It's the Bishop's purse with little but pennies in it."

"Jeeny wore it!"

"Then I'll keep it!"

"No!" M. de Champvallon cried. "I will 'ave it from you!"

"Will you? Will you indeed?" Chedlowe slipped the purse under the breast of his waist-coat. "Will you try to get it?" His voice shook with the foment in him, and M. de Champvallon was near giving him his desire but glanced toward Jinny, who was now some paces in advance of them.

"That poor Bishopp!" he said. "It would be a sad remembrance." Then he was lightly in the saddle again, and, in a moment more, at Jinny's side. "Misterr Chedlowe and I pause' to 'old a council," he told her. "We are in accord. Dear child, will you 'ear what we think?" She inclined her head slightly, not speaking; but he seemed pleased with the sign. "Ah, she listen, so I mus' speak with wisdom! Well, then, the one thing for us to do now is to choose the place where we shall wait." He had been peering through the fog; now he pointed. "Some tree' and bush', I think, to the right. Yes, let us see if we can make a little shelter there per'aps. I do not think there will be any other in'abitants."

"Fuddle-de-diddle!" Mr. Chedlowe said; but followed the Chevalier's lead, as did Jinny. They turned their horses into the copse, pushed through bush and branch to its centre, and there drew rein. For a time they sat silent in the dim grey silence of the place; the underbrush, wet and ragged, rose above their stirrups; twisted elbows of branches crossed thickly above the underbrush, and, though the copse was leafless, it gave hiding. The Chevalier spoke of this cheerfully, though in a low voice.

"Ah, good fortune! That naughty fog is 'ere, too, where we almos' do not need it. Well, I think we would be unseen in this place on a bright day; but now with the fog if we 'ad something to eat and drink we could stay for a week. While we wait I could tell you a tale of 'ow an ancestor of mine 'id 'imself in a carp-pond in the Huguenot Wars, with only 'is nose above the water. Well, it was a very small nose and—"

But he did not tell the tale. "No!" Jinny said in an angry voice, though she held her head down and kept her face from his sight and Chedlowe's, too.

"No!" the Chevalier said instantly. "No tale!"

The copse was still again, so still that a double silence seemed to lie upon it: that of its own grotesque motionlessness coupled with that other inscrutable silence of the fog. The thick and gloomy air grew slowly, slowly gloomier;—when Chedlowe's horse shook his head, clinking the steel of his bit, the unexpected sound was like the crash of a disaster, and Jinny uttered a shivering cry of protest.

"Don't let him do that!" she said sharply to Chedlowe, though she did not look at him.

"Let him!" he echoed. "What's in your vitals, Jinny? How'm I to let or not let a horse shake his head? There's a task to set me! I'd sooner promise to make Tom Colpoys fight. What?" His humor changed and he laughed huskily. "Why, here's a quip I'll carry about the town with me when I'm there again! Which is easier: to let a horse not shake his head or to make Tom Colpoys fight? That'll make 'em merry, when the rest is told, how you and I drubbed him. Lord! If they'll believe it of him! Tom Colpoys! Tom Colpoys that wouldn't bear half the wink of an eye turned away from him! D'you think any'll credit it, Jinny?" He became more thoughtful. "It's to be doubted even though the two of us swear to it, and there's no other means to prove it but by Champvallon, and he's a Frenchman, so wouldn't weigh. If I could take Colpoys with me and beat him again afore 'em, why, that'd be rare and prove it double." He laughed again; then was thoughtful again. "No; we'll never get belief for it, because we can't speak of it, that we saw him here; and Colpoys'll be thought a deadly ruffian no man could mishandle save when he's in his irons, as he will be then unless they deal with him out o' hand afore we're home again. Well, the fault's his own now and not on our hands, Jinny, since he sat there silly, as you told him, when he could 'a' made a good end on it. To my view o' the matter, he's an ass not to choose fighting instead o' waiting for the gallows tree to—"

M. de Champvallon spoke as loudly as he dared. "'Ark! Do I 'ear something yonder?" He had heard nothing except the voice of Chedlowe, which he wished to silence, so after a moment he

said reassuringly, "No; there is nothing." He
leaned toward Jinny. "You still wish not to 'ear
the tale of my ancestor's nose in the Huguenot
Wars?"

"No!"

"No," he said again. "No tale."

"Well, that's a mercy," Chedlowe said, and
pursued a previous train of thought. "No, what
they do with him now he's brought on himself
and our hands are washed of it. What? A man
that sits and takes a beating while the woman
he's daft for takes another!" Mr. Chedlowe
laughed again, once more being reminiscent with
humor. "You went for her roundly, Jinny—ay,
and for him roundlier! Ha, to see you dashing
that little tight fist o' yours into their faces and
rating 'em without pause in the drubbing! You're
strong, too, sweetheart, strong as a little bullock.
'Clack' your fist would say to lip or eye, and
every time left the mark of it. Why, you—"

"Now," M. de Champvallon interrupted
briskly, "I am going to tell you the tale of my
ancestor's nose and the carp-pond at the time of

the Huguenot Wars. 'E was of the 'ouse'old of
Monsieur le duc de Bouillon—"

"Frenchman!" Mr. Chedlowe said, pleased to
let his bursting truculence have its way. "You
babble and gabble while I'm speaking, do you?
Put that finger o' yours on my chin, as you did
to Colpoys, and I'll not wait to see what stomach
you have to go further. Touch me with your finger, Frenchman! Touch me, I say!"

M. de Champvallon felt that his philosophy
threatened him with a treacherous departure.
From the moment of their first acquaintance
Chedlowe had taken the high hand with him in a
lady's presence, had made a contemptuous dis-
like all too plain, had baited him and could never
be counted upon for decent manners ten minutes at a time. At Mally Older M. de Champvallon had placed his finger upon the chin of Tom
Colpoys in Jinny's cause and in the belief that his
action might advance her safety; on his own account he would warmly have preferred the chin
of Mr. Chedlowe. In the copse, now, he looked
anxiously at this preferred chin and feared that
he might tap it in spite of himself; his breath,

indeed, was quicker with a panting thus to assault it, and there was a boiling within him almost impossible to stopper. He muttered, twitched, rubbed a dampening gauntlet across his mouth, then looked at the back of Jinny's hat and was cool again. "I abandon the carp-pond," he said.

But Chedlowe, as if there had been no need in the world for quiet, began to sing in an insulting, full voice.

"Now, folderol-diddle and folderoldol,
'I spit on all Frenchmen!' quod sober Old Noll—"

The Frenchman uttered an exclamation of horror, rose in his stirrups and clapped his hand over the Englishman's mouth. "Silence!"

Chedlowe struck the hushing hand away and in a trice had out his rapier. The Chevalier, thus forced, was as quick; but Jinny turned upon him, and the sight of the gauntness of her face stopped him.

"Good!" she said. "Show me a little blood-letting that's not from a broken lip. To it, bully-boys, to it!"

The Chevalier put up his sword. "Jeeny, Jeeny!" he said, staring at her. "You're not showing me blood from a broken 'eart?"

She put her hands over her face and began to sob lamentably.

CHAPTER XIV

IN THE hall at Mally Older Anne was the first to stir. "Here was a glory!" she said in a whisper; then went to the kitchen, brought water in a basin, laved Colpoys's face and her husband's and, after that, her own. The little tanner was transfigured.

"To have seen this day!" he said, as he rose. "To have seen the light come upon so great a man!"

Colpoys smiled with half of a swollen mouth, stood and put his hand upon Francis's shoulder. "Great for being drubbed? Then we're all three great, and so is any drubbed schoolboy, Francis."

"But we saw the light come—"

Colpoys shook his head. "No."

"But we saw—"

"No, Francis. We were beat because I wouldn't bring worse harm upon you than I took you from. I couldn't chance a hurt to me that would keep me from carrying you to the ship, and so I must sit and be battered and let you and Anne be battered with me. It was the course that cost the least and the following of it was but wisdom. I can't let you think I had my stubborn wisdom from the 'light'."

"No?" Anne said, and she looked not less content. "First thou did say thy spirit could not abide a mishandling; then, when a woman mishandled thee and thou was peaceful, thou did say it was because she was a woman, and what she did to thee couldn't be brooked from a man. Thou did say this was why thy spirit was not truly that of a Friend. Now thou'st borne blows from both a woman and a man and say thy forbearance was but shrewdness. Tell me what was thy thought when the man struck thee?"

"Thought? What I thought? Why, that if he provoked me I'd fight; therefore I mustn't let myself be provoked. Well, not to be provoked, I thought, 'Let him do what he will to my body. Myself, as I must bear in mind, he can't touch— so let him vent himself; there's no provocation.' "

"Yes? Did thou hate him?"

"Why, no," Colpoys said. "I think I didn't."

"Dost thou hate him now?"

"Now? Hate him?" He seemed to examine himself inwardly and to be surprised by a discovery. "Why, no; I think it was Chedlowe's frantic nature to do what he did, and his nature was played on."

Anne beamed upon him. "So! Why did thou bear blows? It was for Francis's good and mine; therefore thou did bear the blows for us. He that struck thee could not touch thee, and that is the light. Hast borne persecution for the sake of others and hast no rancor against thy persecutors. Friend, friend, thou need not speak with the speech of the Friends—that's a little matter—but I tell thee there never was a Friend if thou'rt not one, and Francis said well that this was a great day for him and me. Wilt thou go with us on the ship and come to live among the Friends across the sea?"

"I?"

"There'll be no more Friends brought by the way of Mally Older," Anne said. "She'll see to it. There'll be traps for thee; she's not done with thee."

"Not done with me? After what she's done?"

"No," said Anne. "She'll never be done with thee."

"Never? You think Jinny'll never be done with me?" The compassionate nod of Anne Tanner's head was not needed to deepen the conviction her word "never" had already revealed as within him. Concerning Jinny Wilmot there was a confusion in his mind; but out of the confusion came the one certainty: there was something indissoluble between them that was being brought to light by her tragic misuse of him. More, he saw that this misuse was but part of a war between them that began with his flight from her, and now, after three years, reached its crisis. In this long war he had always been weak-

ened by a recognition, vainly hidden from himself, of the justice of her cause against him, and
he knew, too, that it was within her right to be
indomitable in her assaults upon him and that
the "hard hurt" she said would rid him of her
could not suffice. Nothing could rid him of her
and he knew strangely well that nothing could
rid her of him. Now less than ever could they
be rid of each other, for there existed between
them a new imperishable intimacy, the curious
understanding that is between a wife and a husband when either has beaten the other. Colpoys
set Chedlowe aside as not human and no more
than a cudgel in Jinny's hands; Jinny had done
all the beating, and the man she drubbed had
just told the two Quakers that he bore the drubbing the better for his thought that blows upon
his body were not blows upon himself. He had
thought this and, while the blows fell, was up-
held by the thought; yet now, when Anne said
"never", he wondered if there had been no other
thought and if his passivity had not been a stroke
at Jinny in his war with her—a battle-stroke to
be called the "light" by the two gentle good

souls who suffered with him! Where was the
truth of the motive of a man's any action? Colpoys had neither means nor time to discover the
truth of his own, nor to know in full conscious-
ness why he felt exaltation as he came to an
abrupt great decision. Yet the three-years' war-
rior within him almost put the motive into words
that could have been heard by his mind's ear:
"This deals her a blow that will smart upon her
forever. Ah, she'll know how I strike back!"

What his voice said was, "I'll take ship with
you, Anne and Francis."

Both of them cried out. "Thou'lt come!"

"I will," he said. "If I go to live in the plantations, the ship can still do her work at English
harbors where Friends can sail, and I think
Anne has the right of it that henceforth there'll
be no way through Mally Older. There's cause
for uneasiness other than this new one—a Justice
at Mally Surfeit, a blundering fellow but sus-
picious and evil-tempered towards any not above
him. It's the man the Frenchman spoke of before
you, Anne; he that looked for 'bad people' on the
moor. He comes prying sometimes, and Lecky's

on the watch for him now. If Jinny goes to him with an information against us—and I think she will—my work here's done indeed and I might be hard put to it to keep from gaol. No, I'll come with you and see my last of Mally Older this night." He went to a window and stared out frowningly. "If she and those two with her was not here, I think we'd do well not to wait for the night."

"We slept well last night without a roof over us," Francis said cheerfully. "If the moor's better for us than this house, let us go—"

"Not while she's here to mark how we go or perhaps follow us. I do think the moor's safer for us than the house if the Justice comes this way—safer a hundred fold if she have speech with him. If we could go unseen a little way from the house we'd be in good cover. Two hundred paces from the Mally yonder there's a crack in the earth that is the way I've taken all the others—a ravine that opens in a thicket, and the thicket's deep about its edges for half its length and so tall a man on a horse isn't seen from without it."

"Then where's the peril, friend?" Francis asked.

"First, that we be seen and followed to the thicket and into it. Not followed quickly, we'd have a better assurance of safety, for the ravine leads to a clutter of great stones among trees; and thence onward, to where we'd lie to wait for sun-up and the ship, the way is so rough and lonely we'd be hard to follow in the dark. What frets me most is the open ground 'twixt the house and the Mally and the Mally and the thicket, lest they watch and follow us."

But Francis was confident. "I see no need to fret. If those three stay and sleep early, we go then; or belike they'll sit in the kitchen for supper, and, if they do, we'll go then. If all three of 'em ride forth to seek this prying Justice, we'll go then. But if one ride out for him and the others stay to watch——"

"Yes," Colpoys said. "What then?"

"Well, that'd be a riddle," the tanner admitted. "So let's be ready to put our wits to the solving of it if we must, and do thou, friend, make preparations for the great journey."

"There's none to make beyond my saddle-pack that's ready in the stable, and the burning of letters that might do harm to some if found here."

"Then burn them now," Anne said, "for I think we have reason to go, and quickly."

"Why?" her husband asked. "We must stay until the dame and—"

"Hark!" she said. "Is there a sound anywhere? When folk are about a house or near it, they may lie quiet but there's not this emptiness of all sound. Hark!"

They did as she bade them and felt more than emptiness of sound; they felt that disquieting vacancy of which human beings have a tenuous sense in a place where others of their kind have been but are no more. Francis's mouth fell open before he spoke. "I think they've gone," he murmured, staring at the wall.

"Make sure of it," Colpoys said.

Francis ran out through the kitchen to the stables while Colpoys went to the room where M. de Champvallon had seen the dismal books; but the little tanner was again in the hall when the owner of Mally Older returned to it with a loose bundle of papers.

"Come!" Francis cried. "Come to the stables!"

Colpoys threw the papers upon the fire; then strode after the two Friends. In the stables the three stood in a sharp amazement. "Why, what!" Colpoys exclaimed. "Why should they?"

"Nay," Anne said. "Why did they? Were their horses more jaded than thine?"

"I think not much. All had some rest, and there was not much to choose but for that white of hers yonder. I know him well; he's far better than any I ever had, a Tangier barb. Now, why should she—"

"Be sure of this," Anne said. "She's done it for a hurt to thee."

"But to leave a horse that has few of his like in England, what intent could—"

Anne shook her head. "I can't tell; but I know she's done it wickedly."

Francis was already busy with a saddle. "What horses we ride will not matter so much as that we do ride," he said. "I think it's time we go."

"It's in my mind that you speak the truth,"

Colpoys told him, picked up the woman's saddle Anne had used on the way to Mally Older and carried it to the white horse. "The white is easy under a woman's riding," he said. "There's a cloth on a foreleg; but I think he's not tender there; he lets his weight go on it, and he's the best here. Bring me one of your packs, Anne."

"Here's both!" she said, beside him with them. "Haste! Haste!"

"Haste and more haste!" her husband agreed, and for five minutes the place was busy with scurryings and bucklings; but Anne was upon her saddle, and Colpoys and the tanner were ready to mount, when Lecky came running in at the door, out of breath.

"Master!" he said, when he could. "There's troopers on the moor! I went farther than you bade me—five or six furlong, it might be—and I heard 'em and got close to three that had a man o' the Squire's from Mally Surfeit with 'em. He was to show 'em the way, I knew by their following him."

"To show 'em the way? What way?"

"Hither! Others was off to right and left of 'em, too, I could tell by their calling softly. 'Keep the line o' the net!' one called."

"How nigh are they?"

"You might have time to be across the Mally, Master. They're coming slow and very careful."

"Then it's fast for us and not careful!" Colpoys said, and bestrode the black horse. "Up with you, Francis! Lecky, we leave the house empty; run by my stirrup."

Anne pointed into the fog, as they rode out through the doorway. "Look!" she said. "What's there?" The vapor was thinner and sieved through and through with a yellow light. Anne's voice shook with her dismay. "The fog's breaking with the sunset. Look!"

There was more for them to see than the daunting western glow. A woman on a bay horse came on them, galloping through the moving wisps. She rode straight at them, leaped down, and, with furious strong hands, pulled down Anne Tanner from the white horse, so that those

*Sure of halting the pursuit at least momentarily at
Mally Older.*

When the troopers came up.

two women stood on the ground together, face to face. But they stood so for only an instant.

"Leave my horse! You poor fool, take your own!" Jinny cried, and pushed the Quakeress to the bay. "Up, up, poor fool!"

Not dallying, Anne obeyed the raging husky voice and distraught gesture; but Colpoys spoke to Jinny as two cavaliers, following her, one French and one English, drew rein and slid down beside her.

"Jinny, Jinny, what do you?" Colpoys asked her. "What do you, Jinny?"

"I take my own horse," she said, coming close to him and looking up at him. "I take him because it's death to ride him, and that's what I'll have. We three had sport with Bishop Bourne in London and he's dead of it. When you've carried your she-Quaker to a safer place, come to my hanging."

The eyes of the Chevalier de Champvallon were sometimes less philosophic than he wished them to be. He could have made no honest denial if an enemy had charged that there were sentimental tears in them as he heard Jinny speak,

and still as he saw how she looked at Tom Colpoys and how Colpoys looked at her, M. de
Champvallon could only have explained with
embarrassment that it was a sentimental moment.

Colpoys leaned down, put his hands under
Jinny's arms and lifted her to the saddle-bow before him.

"Gentlemen," he said to the Chevalier and
Chedlowe, "I think you'd best ride with us."

"I think so," the Chevalier admitted, and
turned to his horse; but he had not counted upon
Mr. Chedlowe, who chose this special time to re-
lieve a spleen enlarged beyond mere discomfort.
He pointed to Jinny but thrust a scarlet face
almost against M. de Champvallon's pale one.

"You did this!" Chedlowe cried, and brought
his open hand loudly against the Chevalier's
cheek. "She did all to please you and now here's
the end o't. He's got her! I've beat him and I'll
beat him again; but first I'll beat you! I'll beat
any that hampers me with her!"

"Off! Off!" Colpoys said in a deep voice.

Francis and Anne were already at trot, and

Lecky led them. Colpoys rode fast; the fog swept away in a startling clear sunset. But Colpoys and his friends were well into the ravine when the troopers came up and found the Chevalier de Champvallon restoring his rapier to its sheath, and, in company with a white horse, looking down upon Mr. Chedlowe, who lay flat before him.

CHAPTER XV

THE flitting of the fog after days of grey muffling revealed the moor for miles with all its brown twisting shown beneath a bald green clarity of sky, and the change, so sudden, was as if wrought by some celestial whim; but, to the Chevalier's thinking, such necromancy at this juncture was undesirable, even spiteful. He stood disclosed upon high ground, could not imagine anything more conspicuous than himself and wished that Jinny's barb, Snow, had not been so well trained to stand when his bridle-reins were let fall. The two loose bays, uninterested in the combat between their late riders, had strolled congenially to Mally Older's stables; but Snow proved steadfast, all too tranquil, though now his head was up and he looked doubtfully at the mounts of four approaching troopers. The Chevalier earnestly wished, too, that Snow had been of a different tint, for, although he stood in the sunset purely a golden horse, there could be no doubt that Misterr Bron-age and M. le Colonel Bourne would ignore the simple testimony of their eyes and think him white.

Though he grudged the point, M. de Champvallon perceived that he himself must admit that Snow was white. Other admissions would be necessary, and their selection called upon genius; nevertheless, he was sure of halting the pursuit at least momentarily at Mally Older. To detain it there for as much as half an hour might be to give the fugitives a hope, and, as for the self-sacrifice possibly requisite to that end, he saw no need of any, since he regarded himself as already lost. His visible close association with a white horse, not to speak of what had been done to Mr.

Chedlowe, made for him a position so irretriev-
ably compromising that not even the dazzling
ingenuity of M. de Lauzun (the Chevalier's
cousin who married the King's cousin) could
have explained it.

M. de Champvallon bore with dignity his capture by the troopers. He said not a word when
two of them laid hold of him and took his rapier,
and he merely looked preoccupied when the
leader of this party asked him questions: "Now
which o' ye is the rogue Colpoys, you or him
that's on the ground? D'you hear me, spark? A
fellow that plays his long-sticker as you do, ha'n't
you no tongue? What! No ears neither?" The
Chevalier's absent-mindedness seemed to increase; whereupon the questioner contented himself with a prediction. "Ah, the Col'nel will have
speech quick enough from you, my bully!" he
said. "Wills and Smith, have this cocky-boy into
the stables, find rope and strap and truss him and
if the female's hid there, truss her, too. George,
hold the white horse here; I'll ride to the Col'nel."

With the galloping away of this trooper, the
meditation of M. de Champvallon deepened, and,

marching submissively to the stables, he there endured in continued silence the ignominies commanded for him. Colonel Bourne and Mr. Brunnage were together, meanwhile, at the other side of Mally Older, directing the encircling movement and so eager to have it completed quickly, since the air had surprised them by becoming transparent, that the messenger could not instantly gain their attention.

"No time, Hawes, no time!" Bourne said. "Are your three fellows up along the Mally?"

"They are, Col'nel; but—"

"Later, man! Later! Brunnage, call to your guides to bring those with 'em in closer. Call openly—no fear now! The fish are in the net."

"If the house is the net, only the female's hid in it, Col'nel," the trooper said, persisting. "The two men was in the open when we had sight of 'em."

At this, both the Colonel and the Justice listened. "What!" Brunnage cried. "Gone away? Gone away?"

"No, that they're not!" Hawes told them with emphasis. "We've taken 'em, Col'nel, me and

Dirty George and Wills and Prodigious Smith.
I've been to a playhouse but never see a prettier
thing. The fog spun off and there up a slope, as
if we was in the pit, we saw the nicest long-stab
fighting that ever eyes had pleasure of!"

"What? Who was—"

"The two he-rogues o' the three we've rode so
far to catch, Col'nel. I never thought to see highway boys so noble in their work! They must 'a'
fell out from some cause that come too hot atwixt
'em as they was making into the house, and
thought the open was better ground for 'em than
where walls'd hamper 'em. It's a pity you wasn't
on that side o' the house with us, Col'nel. You'd
'a' had your pleasure of it, if I know you!"

"Not I, Hawes," the Colonel said. "I'd 'a'
feared they'd chouse me from the hanging of
'em. You hold 'em both, do you? And where's
the female?"

"She must 'a' run indoors to hide; but her
white horse was there like a good beast, and you'll
have her easy enough—under a bed or up a chim-
bley, belike, by this time."

"Good!" the Colonel said, and his face was

exultant. "You'll have ale, and more, too, for this, Hawes. Go on and call in our wings—every man into the house! Take the woman and all papers. Brunnage, we'll ride back to have sight o' the two bloody rogues where they stand."

"Ay, sir," Hawes said. "But the slain one's not standing and t'other's being trussed in the stables."

"One's killed? The bloody cheat!"

The Colonel loosed a clamor of swearing, and Hawes thought best to ride upon his errand before there should be right suspicion of him for delaying interruption of the playhouse spectacle because of his pleasure in it. He departed suddenly, and Bourne and Brunnage rode round the house, dismounted and went to look at the prostrate figure near the Mally.

Mr. Brunnage was amazed. "Why, here's finery! Fie, fie! To think that rogues should ride so fine! Not Colpoys, this one, and no Quaker neither by the looks of him."

"Quaker!" Bourne cried, his eyebrows bushed. "Him!"

"You know him, Bourne?"

"I've no acquaintance with him; but he's known to me as one Rafe Chedlowe, a fellow pointed at in London as of such frenzy in his humors that many believe his wits gone. Queer Quakery here, Brunnage!"

Mr. Brunnage admitted that the matter was perplexing, and, glancing curiously at the white horse, found more to puzzle him. "By blood and bones!" he said, and the Colonel, staring at Snow's saddle, said worse. "But looky now," Brunnage argued;—"without information this is beyond us. This Chedlowe can't be questioned. What we deal with is the highwaymanry and the Quaker plot. That's Colpoys, and Colpoys, thanks to me, we hold trussed. So let's after the woman and her quick confession to confront him with!"

"And quick hanging thereupon," the Colonel said, and began to shout to the soldiers who were riding in from all points of the partly formed circle. "Into the house with ye! The first to find the female and bring her to me'll have double ale. In with ye! In with ye!"

The troopers dropped from their horses and

scrambled for the reward; thunderously they rummaged the house, pounded the walls, sounded the chimneys and even the thatch. The Colonel and the Justice took the hall for their own searching and easily satisfied themselves that it concealed nothing; but Hawes and other heavy-stepping men brought the information that nothing was concealed anywhere. The Colonel bawled at them: "Get me her! Get me her! How could she be gone? She's here, cheese-heads!"

"Nah, nah, Col'nel. There's a rub here, sir," Hawes said, and scratched a bristling chin. "More than one rub, if you'll put your mind to it, Col'nel. The word's passed round among us all since noon we was to catch a Quaker name o' Colpoys and a he and she Quaker with him, the three that did the ill work on the Bishop. Well, here's no Quakers and no female neither. We've catched a dead man and a dumb man, both dressed like spry gallants, and no black horse at all and nobody with a black face—"

"Cheese-head!" the Colonel shouted. "Is there no water in the world to wash with?"

"Ah, there may be water," Hawes admitted.

"But here's a rub that rubs me: the woman we follow was riding a man's saddle like a man, and the white barb yonder has a woman's saddle on him. Now what—"

The Colonel swore at a bellow. "Fetch me this Colpoys! I'll rub him with these rubs and see't he has the female out o' where she lies, soon enough. Fetch the bloody rogue!"

Nothing is more difficult for a man than to appear graceful when shackled and mishandled. The straps about M. de Champvallon's ankles permitted him to advance of his own will not more than six inches at a step; his elbows were pinioned behind him by ropes and a stout stick, and, as he came into the hall at Mally Older, he was hurried, nudged, bumped, pushed about and even thrust forward from behind. Moreover, this entrance was accomplished to an accompaniment of objurgation; yet his air all the while was of a noble modesty so meet for the occasion and so consistently maintained that it must have been less natural than calculated. He remained silent in a din to which Mr. Brunnage's exclamations loudly contributed, and it was not, indeed, until the Colonel had shouted down all others that the Chevalier could have been heard if that had been his desire. Big Bourne glowered down upon him with bloodshot eyes.

"Ah, villain, villain Colpoys, I have you! Where is she, villain Colpoys?"

"Now looky, Bourne!" Brunnage cried, "I have authority here, and I tell you this—"

"Easy, Brunnage!" the Colonel said, not moving his gaze from the captive. "Which'll you have, Colpoys, a twist o' the neck afore you speak or after, or both afore and after—the last if you make me wait two winks o' your bloody eye!"

The Chevalier comprehended that there are times when even silence may be overdone; he made the semblance of a ceremonious bow to Mr. Brunnage and spoke to him. "Misterr Bron-age, until now there was nobody to w'ich a gentleman could speak. Since I am a captive I 'ave the honor to surrender myself to you."

"Easy, Brunnage!" Bourne said again, forestalling another effort on the part of the Justice to make himself heard. "Now, Colpoys, what finical manner o' speech d'you think to practise

on me? Wheedling, is it? Wills, wheedle one of
his thumbs back against his wrist for me, will
you!"

Undoubtedly M. de Champvallon would have
suffered this excruciation if Mr. Brunnage had
been less thick-headed. Impressions lodging for
even a little time under the Justice's great periwig became convictions; hours earlier he had
become convinced that M. de Champvallon, a
friend of M. de Grammont, was indeed Musseer
Shove-along, a friend of Musseer de Grammont.
Mr. Brunnage retained forever all of his convictions, and this was one of them; moreover, he
believed that he'd implanted within the breast
of Musseer Shove-along a grateful desire to be of
service to him through the mediation of Musseer
de Grammont. Concerning other convictions of
Mr. Brunnage's, it may be said that there were
now foments in the turgid cauldron of his mind,
where heavy acids seemed to steam in conflict
with indissolubles: Colpoys and a female and a
male Quaker, and a bay horse and a black horse
and a white horse (under a man's saddle) were
guilty of the assault upon episcopacy, and, now

that the sunset faded, must be at Mally Older;
yet here instead were Musseer Shove-along and a
dead witless gentleman of London, two bay
horses and (the one thing that should of right
be here) the white horse—but the white horse
wore a woman's saddle! Out of the foments,
Brunnage picked a single fact and clung to it;
Musseer Shove-along was the friend of Musseer
de Grammont, and the Colonel was confronted
by a Justice who made a ponderous to-do, could
browbeat more easily than be browbeaten, and,
roaring, stopped the thumb-twisting.

"French, is he?" the Colonel roared back.
"Shove-along not Colpoys? What of it, since he's
catched red-handed?"

"How red-handed? He's no Quaker, and 'twas
Quakers bled your brother. Is a Quaker a Frenchman? Tell me this: Saw you ever a Quaker
dressed in rose velvet and—"

"Quaker! Quaker! Can't a Quaker change his
dress to do a murder, Brunnage? Can't he make
pretense to be a Frenchman? Can't he—"

"I ask your pardon," M. de Champvallon said.
"Since Misterr Bron-age speak with you, sir, I

think you may be an officer of the guard and so
I will speak with you myself. I—"

"You will, will you?" the Colonel cried.
"You'll speak with me? Ay, that you will!
Where's your female?"

"Mine? I 'ave none," the Chevalier replied,
with melancholy. "No female."

"No? You was with her and a man at Littlefield, and the three of ye rode into Wanton
Mally at sun-up!"

"Pardon," M. de Champvallon said. "There
was no sun and no moon, and I was with nobody
but a fog." He paused for an instant only, and
then put his opinion of Mr. Brunnage to the
test. "Sir, by the advice of Monsieur de Grammont I wish' to improve myself by learning the
custom' and 'abit' of the great English people,
and now I 'ave even more to forgive 'im; for, to
commence what 'is advice 'as done to me, yesterday evening I did come into this Vanton Mallee
and am los' all the night, and then—"

"What! Bloody rogue, you pretend you was on
the moor all night?"

M. de Champvallon looked at the Colonel

steadily. "Sir, I will ask you very soon to make amend' for some word' you speak to me. At this moment I only inquire if Misterr Bron-age still wish' me to remain 'is frien'. Misterr Bron-age know' very well who I am and that I was all the night alone and los' in this desolation."

"So I do, so I do," Brunnage said promptly, in good faith. "I tell you, Bourne, he's Musseer Shove-along, a Frenchman. He was on the moor all night because I found him deep into it this morning, lost and alone, and I set him on his way to the Stag's Horn at——"

"The Stag's Horn? So!" the Colonel cried triumphantly. "Then how comes it he's catched here at Colpoys's house?"

"But he'll tell you," Brunnage said. "There's a cloud on the matter and how can we pierce to the truth of it if you'll not let him talk? Speak up, Musseer Shove-along. How is it you're not at the Stag's Horn on the King's Highway where I sent you but instead are here at a place of ill repute, this Mally Older, slaying yonder Ched-lowe and in company with yon white horse that was at the laying low o' the most becoming prel-

ate in England? You can but see, yourself, Musseer Shove-along, the thing has a mischievous look
and cries for some explanation."

The Chevalier saw this indeed; but thought
best not to admit that he saw it. In London his
acquaintance with the unfortunate Chedlowe
had begun on the afternoon of the great mis-
adventure, and, recalling this fact, he looked at
Mr. Brunnage with an air of perplexed inquiry.
"You say, Misterr Bron-age, Mallee Olda? What
is that?"

"This house, Musseer."

"Ah! And you speak the name Ched— What
is that name you say, Misterr Bron-age?"

"Chedlowe. Chedlowe's him you fought with
and finished."

"Ah, Chedlowe." The Chevalier shook his head
painfully, yet made use of the opportunity; for,
with every word he uttered, speaking as slowly
as he dared, his heart heard a horse take one more
step—the horse that carried Jinny Wilmot.
"That poor, poor man!" he said. " 'E surprise'
me very much. 'E use 'is weapon like a gentleman
train' in the bes' school of arms. I think at some

time 'e practise' with a French master, because
one time, two time', three time' 'e pass' my guard
and—"

"Now, now, Musseer Shove-along!" Brunnage
remonstrated. "You was to tell us why you're
here and not at the Stag's Horn where you—"

"I lose myself again," the Chevalier said with
some promptness. "When I leave you this morning, Misterr Bron-age, I follow that road a
distance; then all at once I do not see it but I see
a window w'ich show the light of a warm fire
burning. Well, you can be sure that did not displease me, because I was not warm and also very
wet. Well, I knock on the door and a servant
come. 'E say 'is master is not 'ere; but I tell 'im
I would like some food. So I eat a little food, and
then I go to sleep. See! There is that bench there
by the chimney, and the fire was pleasant. A man
who 'as been los' all night in this Vanton Mallee,
I tell you when 'e 'as some food and wine 'e is
goin' to sleep as long as 'e can if there is a bench
by a warm fire. A man in fatigue and wet with
a fog and feeling a strong 'unger, well, when a

such man 'as food and warmth to dry 'imself—"

Colonel Bourne unleashed the voice of fury,
while M. de Champvallon, pleased with the time
gained for thought and for those in flight,
waited with an air of patience; but Mr. Brunnage, not pleased at all, interrupted as soon as he
could be audible.

"Chut! Col'nel! You've no experience o' wit-
nesses, man. Leave it to me. So you fell asleep
here by the fire, did you, Musseer Shove-along?
You waked afore the fog lifted, did you?"

"Lifted? Well, there was a fog—"

"So. Afore it lifted. What waked you?"

"What did?" The Chevalier seemed to rumi-
nate. "Well, I cannot tell 'ow long I was asleep;
but I was in a condition of fatigue and—"

"We know, we know! What waked you?"

"I think it was a sound," the Chevalier said.
"I think I 'eard a sound and that when I 'eard
the sound I woke."

"Ha! A sound. Was it the sound of Colpoys
speaking?"

"Colpoys?" the Chevalier asked. "I do not

know 'im, and the sound was not the sound of a
voice. I cannot say what it was; but I think there
mus' 'ave been a sound, because I woke. Well,
I stretch' myself and I think to myself, 'Now I
will go on my travel' again. I will ask the servant
to tell me 'ow I can go to the Stag' 'Orn where
Misterr Bron-age was so kind to send me.' So I
call for the servant. I shout. Then I go to look
for 'im, and there is nobody 'ere. Then I go to
the stable', saddle my 'orse myself and ride out
before the 'ouse to see if I can discover that road
again, because I am sure it is not very far away.
Then, while I am looking for it, I see those three
people."

"What!" the Colonel cried. "You saw
three—"

But Brunnage's startled voice prevailed.
"Three! You say you came upon three people?
Who were they?"

M. de Champvallon seemed surprised that the
Justice did not recognize them. "Why, those
three bad people you tol' me of."

"What! What!"

"Those three bad people," the Chevalier repeated. "When I see that they are on a black 'orse, a bay 'orse and that one is dress' like a woman on a white 'orse—"

"*Dressed* like a woman!" Brunnage exclaimed. "Dressed *like* a woman!"

"Oh, yes; it is a man dress' like a woman, and all three—" Too eager in this composition, he was upon the point of describing the three figures as shrouded in black cloaks and with soot upon their faces; but in time to save himself he remembered dreadful evidence to the contrary lying near the Mally. "And it mus' be all three 'ave wash' away the black," he said in a sickly voice, after a brief hesitation. "Also it mus' be they throw away their black cloak'. But I was sure they were those bad people. Misterr Bronage, when I 'ad wander' all night on the moor and you discover' me in the morning, you say to me, 'Well,' you say—"

The Colonel stamped his foot so hard that his great boot put a mark upon the floor. "Now sting me with vipers!" he said. "Call me every name in the rainbow and wash me with hell-flame! How long do we stand here listening to this gibble-gabble? If he will not out with it—"

"Tush! Tush!" Mr. Brunnage interrupted; but besought the Chevalier to be more crisply direct. "Here's the dark hard upon us, and, if there's more pursuits to be carried on, haste's needful as you can see for yourself, Musseer Shove-along."

"Well, I will tell you," the Chevalier said. "I do not know everything, so I cannot tell you everything. A man can tell what 'e know'; but, if 'e is ask' to tell what 'e do not know, 'e cannot tell it unless 'e would be willing to say what might not be true, and then per'aps some people would belief 'im; but there would be others w'ich would think, 'No, no; this man 'e say what is not the truth.' And so—" He was addressing himself to the Justice but kept a wary white of his eye toward Bourne, and impressions gathered by this indirect vision warned him that to push delay further might not be helpful. "And so," he continued, with prudent haste, "and so when I ride out of the stable' on my bay 'orse, those three bad people, they see me and they ask me where is that road."

"The Mally?" Brunnage said. "Colpoys knows

the Mally like any poacher. Yet there afore his
own house he asks you to find it for him? Was
he the one dressed like a woman?"

"I do not know because I 'ave never see 'im.
This one like a woman, 'e 'as blue eye', each between two brown bag'; 'e 'as a blue thick nose
and very 'airy on the chin. Another you tell me
is name' Ched—ah, Chedlowe, and the third
one I 'ear the one like a woman call 'im Deek."

" 'Deek'? Dick!" Hawes interposed. "It could
be Clouterly Dick that was with Old Mobb when
they robbed Mistress Carwell on Bagshot Heath.
Clouterly Dick's a bloody-eyed, brown—"

"What, Big-mouth?" Brunnage shouted.
"Will you put in your say while I'm question-
ing?" He returned his attention to the Chevalier.
"You say they asked you for the Mally?"

"Yes, they ask' me; but, well, I do not know
where that road is, myself, so 'ow can I tell them?
More, I do not wish to tell them, because I know
they are bad people, as I 'ave been tol', and so I
say, 'Well, I do not know where that road is.'
Well, the man w'ich pretend to be a woman, 'e
was looking on the ground and 'e say to them 'e

think 'e see the road now, and they tell me they would like to take my 'orse."

"Yours?" Brunnage asked heavily. "They said they would take your horse? Slow here, Musseer Shove-along, slow, lest our minds be mazed. Slow!"

" 'Slow'?" the Colonel inquired, with bitterness. "He's not slow enough for you, Brunnage?"

"Now looky, Col'nel; here's a thought I'd not had if I'd pushed him faster. They was cunning, those three, and thought to take his horse from him so't with three less marked, and the white one left behind, pursuit would be confused. How was it, Musseer Shove-along? Tell us carefully of their appearance, of their speech with you and what they did."

"Well, I will do it," the Chevalier responded. In diplomacy he was seldom a man for half measures, and, although under certain circumstances untruth was abhorrent to his nature, he reserved to himself the right to select the circumstances. As diffusely as he could, for all the while his heart heard the stepping of that horse carrying two, he disclosed an adventure necessarily piece-

meal in the narrative, since it was constructed in
his mind in that fashion, bit by bit. Nevertheless,
the impromptu was masterly, and, as the genius
of Jinny Wilmot had painted upon the imagina-
tions of the harriers a definite picture of their
quarry, so now the inspiration of the Chevalier
seized upon that same picture and retouched it.
Three rash and wicked figures he made vivid, one
the unlucky spark all had seen sprawled by the
Mally, another a brown ruffian called "Deek",
and the third a bulbous, blue-nosed, hairy-
chinned ruffian dressed like a woman and riding
the white horse. Two items, the fallen Chedlowe
and the famous horse, were actually visible from
the windows; the Chevalier made "Deek" and
the bulbous ruffian almost as plain in the minds
of his listeners. "Well, look for yourself—yonder
is the 'orse and there is that poor Ched—Chedlowe." That is to say, he proved the elephant by
the elephant's tail.

Of his two principal hearers, the Justice was
the more befogged, for Mr. Brunnage could not
divest himself of his Quaker conception; but
Bourne had ridden all the way from London to

Wanton Mally with his mind's eye fixed upon
three disguised criminals, two of whom might
easily be realized in the portraits of "Deek" and
the bulbous one. When Brunnage interrupted
doggedly, "But Colpoys, Colpoys! I find no Colpoys in all this", the Colonel turned upon him.

"Let be! Let be! Man, you're Colpoys-fud-
dled; there's light coming here and more riding
for us to do to-night, I think. On with it,
Frenchman! What after all this talk you say they
had with you about the taking of your horse?
What was the action, the action?"

"Well, I will tell you. This Deek and the one
you say 'is name is Chedlowe, they ride up on
both side' of me, and Chedlowe, 'e put 'is 'and
agains' me to push me off my 'orse, and Deek,
'e grasp the bridle. Well, I could not permit a
such impertinence, and Chedlowe, 'e seem' to me
more like a gentleman, so I ask if something cannot be done and 'e say 'e will do it—'e like very
much to fight me for my 'orse. Well, Deek and
the one dress' like a woman, they laugh but they
are angry and they say no, they are in 'aste and
the fog grow' thin, and they reproach Ched-

lowe for being a madman; they wish' 'e was not with them and 'e would not be if they 'ad better acquaintance with 'im before what they did in London. I 'ear them say that, myself, and they tell 'im also—"

" 'Tell him! Tell him'!" the Colonel shouted. "What did they *do?*"

"Well, 'e say 'e wish' to fight like a gentleman and will do nothing until that is done; so we all jump down from our 'orses, and the engagement commence' between us two, for 'e insist' that is the way it is to be done. Well, I can tell you 'e did very well, much better than I thought possible. And then, pfui! all at once there is no fog; Deek and the one like a woman are galloping away on my 'orse and the black 'orse, and the 'orse of Chedlowe is walking to the stable'. One moment, two moment', three moment'— per'aps more—and I see some soldier' coming slowly; then in a little while I am successful with that poor Chedlowe. I tell you 'e press' me very 'ard—'e is too fierce so that 'e is careless—but in other respec' excellent and with a wris' one of the mos' powerful I did ever—"

"Tah! Tah!" the Colonel interrupted. "You say the other two rode away on—"

"Why, here's a rub!" Hawes made bold to intervene. "He says Chedlowe's horse went to the stables. Well, that's one; but there's two bay horses, saddled, standing there. What make you o' that, sir? And how come the female saddle on the white un, when all accounts we had by the way was that the one dressed like a woman rode like a man? There's the rub o' the horses and the rub o' the saddle and the—"

Mr. Brunnage agreed with emphasis that there were rubs. "Ay, and looky, there's the rub o' Colpoys and how he's in it, and the rub o' the she-Quaker and a Quaker man, how they be in it with him. Ah, and where's Colpoys's servant Lecky, why's he not here? To my thinking there's rubs that leaves five to be catched yet, Quaker Colpoys and two others and this Clouterly Dick and the debauched one dressed like a—"

"Rubs! Rub me with brimstone!" the Colonel cried, and added items to brimstone. "We followed three; one's dead and two's to be catched. Which way'd they ride, Musseer Shove-along?"

"That." The Chevalier pointed in the direction followed by the Mally as it went toward the King's Highway. "I think they follow the road if they can."

"North! North we ride. Hawes, loose him enough to set him on a horse; we carry him with us."

"Pardon," the Chevalier said, as Hawes took the straps from his ankles. "I will ride with you, sir; but there was a question of amend' for—"

"Amends!" The Colonel bawled at him. "Thank me for not hanging you straight off! Cheese-heads!" he bawled even louder at his staring troopers. "To horse, cheese-heads! How long'll ye wait? To the north and ride spread in a sweep. Bring the Frenchman and on with ye! To the north, cheese-heads, to the north!"

M. de Champvallon came out into the gathering twilight, melancholy, his elbows aching with strain and his heart with loss; yet he was somewhat contented with himself. A long way to the west Colpoys was riding with Jinny Wilmot meek upon his saddle-bow.

CHAPTER XVI

THE dressing-gown of M. de Grammont was of magnificent black and
gold and scarlet Venetian brocade; the dressing-
gown of his visitor was a China silk, lovingly
colored in peach and a subtle green. The two
French gentlemen sat at an elegant small table,
which offered them fragrantly their morning
chocolate, and M. le Chevalier de Champvallon
enjoyed the luxury of again using his native
tongue.

"From what I have told you," he said, "you
see without doubt that I speak English facilely

enough to make myself well misunderstood."
His face, upon which there were some delicate
new traces, imprints of new experience, showed
that he suffered a slight increase of an inward
dolor; the philosophic smile no longer graced his
lips. "From first to last it is certain that she misunderstood me—most of all at the last. I think
it must be the fault of their language in which so
little can be expressed. I should have prepared
myself better. My dear de Grammont, you told
me to study the customs and habits of these
people. Why did you not advise me to learn first
something of their art and belles-lettres?"

"My dear friend!" de Grammont said, surprised. "Do you know someone who has read an
English book?"

"No, certainly; but I think I should have done
well to be the first to peruse such a thing. One
would not look to find a Racine among these
people, no; but though there would be without
doubt an awkwardness of expression and a schol-
astic lack in their poesy I am sure there would be
poesy, for I have discovered that some of them
have a tragic sort of singing in them. Her very

being was made of this. She was herself a poem written not in ink but in a fiery radiance—and, as for me, I went too near, and now am but a very little heap of embers."

M. de Grammont laughed his noiseless laugh and poised his cup of chocolate near his nose, testing the aroma. "Ah, what a man you are! You come to me and ask for the new wild life; I give you what you desire and now, in a month, you return declaring that you are the ashes made by a poem. Believe me, I am all sympathy; but, in the midst of my pain for you, I trust you are going to let me smile a little. A man who plays with the whirlwind and then declares he has been injured by a poem—"

"I will declare worse than that," M. de Champvallon said mournfully. "I have told you she misunderstood me and she did, because she did not even give me enough serious attention to perceive that I am an animal a little unusual—a man capable of ecstasies of admiration for what can never be his, a man willing to make the utmost sacrifices for what would never even know that he made them—but I confess that for a

time I also misunderstood her. I thought it was
her avarice in love that would not let this Colpoys go; but I was wrong, as I knew when I saw
the passion with which she first struck him upon
the mouth. I have just said I would declare
worse to you than that I have been seared by a
poem. It is this: my suffering has been caused by
a woman agonized to possess a soul."

"How, how! Souls? Now you speak to me of
souls?"

"I do," M. de Champvallon replied with a sorrowful firmness. "In the world there is nothing
more desperate than the love of a woman for a
man who can give her a soul, or, if she have one,
for the man who can save it. The ferocity of my
sweet Jeeny for that strange Colpoys was because
there was a perception that he held in his hand
immortal life for her, and if he did not give it
she was lost. She beat and bruised him to get it
and found herself only the more lost. Ah, that
was a mysterious sight!"

"What! My dear Champvallon! Mysterious to
see a jealous woman beating a man?"

The Chevalier shook his head, and for a mo-

ment a wistful perplexity seemed to possess him.
"No; I am speaking now of three people sitting
upon a bench and, without lifting their hands
or with any appearance of anger, permitting
themselves to be cruelly used. It was a strange
sight and I must tell you that it has a very strange
effect. Quecka, they are called, and their inac-
tion has a singular power upon people who see it.
I felt it myself—a very strong emotion in me—
and, as for my sweet Jeeny, it killed her. She was
lost then unless she could find something to do
that would give her a power to match that singular one of the Quecka. So she rode back to
make the sacrifice and pull that pretty woman
she hated down from her white horse, as I have
told you."

"As you have told me indeed!" M. de Grammont murmured, with a chuckle politely imperceptible. "Éh, what comedy!"

"Comedy!"

"You do not see it in that light, dear Champvallon? The rival rides away with the lady in his
arms, while the hero, facing a double death, re-
mains behind to fight a madman and perhaps be

hanged in order to cover the retreat; then, becoming prisoner, tells a thousand lies for that same purpose! You do not call this comedy?"

"Ah, yes," M. de Champvallon said, and his depression still increased. "In that light I fear I must; I perceive I have played not the hero but the part of the faithful buffoon. The hero—well, at my first sight of that extraordinary man, Colpoys, I had a premonition that the rôle was his. I regret to say that I immediately perceived in him a personage of some visible grandeur. There were gestures of his one does not forget; the action with which he lifted that sweet Jeeny to his saddle—"

"But, yes, to his saddle," M. de Grammont interrupted. "You have not told me how the matter of the saddles and the other bay horse was settled. Éh, there was a problem for your Bronage and Monsieur le Colonel Bourne! What did they make of it?"

"Nothing."

"How! You tell me they made nothing of it? When such questions arise, they must be answered and so how could—"

"Listen, my friend," the Chevalier de Champvallon said. "The Abbé de Baucy went to visit
his father, the Maréchal, at Baucy-le-Pont, and
one night the old man heard a noise outside the
door of his bedchamber, lighted a candle, opened
his door and found a young doe in the corridor,
which was on the second floor. The Abbé de
Baucy was in the next room; he came out, too,
with a candle, and they began to talk about the
manner in which such a marvel could have happened. They went downstairs, talking about it
all the time, and they found the doors bolted,
and also they could not believe that the doe had
mounted the grand stairway. 'To-morrow,' said
the Maréchal, 'we will go and tell the King about
this doe', and the Abbé agreed, and they went on
talking more and more until at times the conversation became an argument. Each one would
try to tell the other how such a thing could have
happened; but would always become entangled
with impossibilities set forth by the other. Well,
they talked all night and into the next morning,
until finally they were so tired of the subject that
they had the doe carried down into the park and

agreed that the only thing to do was to forget this abominable animal and never to speak of her again or they would die of fatigue. You comprehend me, my friend?"

M. de Grammont looked doubtful. "Not entirely, I fear."

"No?" the Chevalier said. "Well, Monsieur le Colonel Bourne and my good Bron-age kept me with them when we rode from the house of Colpoys, and all the time they were talking of the other saddled bay horse and of the woman's saddle, and I could tell them nothing at all except what I had already told them."

"Éh, but your Bron-age and the Colonel Bourne spoke also of the two naughty robbers you were following—your famous brown man, Deek, and the other with the eye-bags and dressed like a woman?"

"At times, and when we would come upon the peasants who were watching the borders of the moor; but then, after every disappointment, they would again begin to talk of the great mystery. The Colonel Bourne wished to know how a man dressed like a woman could ride a woman's saddle like a man, since the saddle had only one stirrup, and Bron-age would tell him it could be done. Then the Colonel Bourne would say, 'Yes, for a moment but not all the way from London to Vanton Mallee, and why would he do it, and why has Deek ridden the black horse away from Mallee Olda when there was another bay horse, and why was there yet another bay horse, saddled, in the stables?' I have simply to tell you that we rode all night on Vanton Mallee and the detestable roads and country about that place of my martyrdom, and all the time those two gentlemen were talking of the woman's saddle and the bay horses, and so were their peasants and soldiers, until no one knew whether to perish of a tired body or fatigue of that subject. There is such a thing as exhausting a topic beyond its power of revival; for all of us the bay horses and the woman's saddle became the doe of Baucy-le-Pont, and by morning the good Bronage and Monsieur le Colonel Bourne were of such a temper that to speak to them of a horse or a saddle, except as something to forget in bed, was dangerous."

"And you, my friend? Was it not at last the occasion when even Champvallon was willing to go to bed?"

"It had been a long night and very cold," the Chevalier said apologetically. "At sunrise we were shivering near the house of Misterr Bron-age and he refused to continue the search until he had some food and sleep—I must ask you to exert yourself a little for him with the King, my dear de Grammont, for he was very anxious to be of service to me. He insisted upon taking me into his house with him, and I think he saved my life. That is to say, if the Colonel Bourne had taken me with his party, as he wished, my peril would have been very great. He and his soldiers were all nearly dead; but someone came and told him that two people like the two I had described were at a tavern six leagues to the north, and, while Misterr Bron-age and I were warm in bed, all the others went to arrest the rascals. My friend, that affair was a disaster."

"For you, Champvallon?"

"No," the Chevalier said. "For the Colonel Bourne. They plodded all the way to that tavern, surrounded it and went in to arrest Deek and his friend. Well, there they were, those two!"

"No, no! Do not forget that they were the creations of the imagination of a malicious Don Quixote called the Chevalier de Champvallon!"

"This is not a fantasy," the Chevalier said. "I am telling you the truth. There in that tavern sat two people at breakfast so much like Deek and the other that there was a great deal of trouble and commotion in the tavern before it could be proved that the man dressed like a woman was really a woman, and, from what I heard one of those poor soldiers later say, the angriest one ever seen in England. People who knew her and her husband came from everywhere in the village where the tavern stands, and when the Colonel was obstinate she became so dangerous, and so were other women who knew her, that the Colonel Bourne and his soldiers came away in great disorder and rode back to the house of Misterr Bron-age in an unbelievable state of mind. They were almost unable to sit their saddles; but the Colonel Bourne held me responsible for everything, and his rage against me was so great I think he would have made matters very embarrassing for me then, except for a circumstance. This was at noon and I had just risen."

M. de Grammont inclined his head, a gesture of satiric approbation. "Ah, yes; you were refreshed and so could create the circumstance that preserved you."

"No," the Chevalier said gravely, and for a moment struggled with an inward distaste. "The body of that poor madman had been brought to the churchyard near the house of Bron-age, and, when the Colonel Bourne arrived, the purse of the prelate, his brother, was shown him, taken from the garments. This was the circumstance that obliged the last suspicions against me to succumb and produced the triumph of Bron-age in upholding me."

"Ah, that unfortunate Colonel! His anger subsided?"

"Subsided! My dear de Grammont, at the very moment when my innocence was thus established, a fisherman came to say a fine black horse without any saddle or bridle had been found wander-

ing near the sea, and the Colonel Bourne cursed
the poor man and swore that if he was ever
spoken to again of horses or saddles he would de-
capitate the person who mentioned them. With
the last strength left in him, he made an uproar,
and then, with all that feeling against horses in
his soul, collapsed in sleep in Misterr Bron-age's
stable among many of those quadrupeds."

"I begin to share his feeling," M. de Grammont said. "When he woke, his chagrin may have
been lessened by the news that his brother was
more fortunate than Misterr Chedlowe and is
now every day better; but the outrageous mystery of the horses will haunt him forever, and so
it will me if you do not tell me why the black
horse was found abandoned and—"

"Ah! Ah!" M. de Champvallon interrupted,
exclaiming sorrowfully. "There you touch my
wound too roughly, dear friend. Do you remember Lannois? He fell in love with Mademoiselle
Bluet, that brilliant, pretty cripple, and for
eighteen years he devoted himself to the care of
her, making every poignant sacrifice for her, re-
ceiving nothing and asking only to believe that

he lived in her thoughts. Then she died, and, weeping, Lannois began to read her diaries and hundreds and hundreds of long letters the handsome rascal musketeer, Crenan, had returned to her on her death-bed. Lannois read and read and read, and, when he finished those weeks of reading, his heart was dead and dried in his breast. In all those volumes of her eighteen years of writing, never once could he find so much as his name even mentioned. Ah, me! I know what he felt."

"But I ask you of the black horse—"

"You ask me and I cannot tell you. My sweet Jeeny let herself be borne away toward the sunset and was lost to my sight in a devouring thicket. Since then—nothing! Not a word to me! It was a vanishment and I cannot tell where they went or where that Colpoys keeps her—perhaps in one of those warm clouds that lay in the western sky toward which they rode. My friend, my friend, in all the thousands of words that she utters to him, my broken heart, listening, hears never once the name of de Champvallon!"

The Chevalier's voice was as exquisite as his person; when he spoke of his broken heart, that rich light voice of his became broken-hearted, too, but musically so, and M. de Grammont, deeply amused, offered what comfort he could. "Since all that she says is addressed to another," he suggested, "isn't it a solace to believe that if she never utters your name in his presence she has a secret pleasant reason for her reticence? When our hearts are broken it is our duty to console ourselves with such reassurances, so that we may regain the amiability to look about us again before we miss the passing by of too many pretty faces."

" 'Pretty faces'," the Chevalier repeated, with a somberness that seemed to drape the very words in purple. "Pretty faces! My life is a vase that has been transfigured by holding in it a great flaming passion-flower. When such a vase has been ravished of such a bloom and is grey and empty, do you offer to place in it a bouquet of little pink roses?"

"Éh, well, let us not altogether despise roses, poor vase! But before I offer them I present two morsels of news."

"Of her? But that is impossible!"

"No, one morsel is of her, though, hélas! my poor Champvallon, not from her. Her guardians came yesterday to tell the King that Meestress Jeeny Feelmotte has been for days where they can by no means find her, and that they now believe a rumor that she has eloped from London with a man named Colpoys—at which the King laughed aloud!"

"Ah! Ah!" the Chevalier exclaimed, with bitterness. "Kings laugh too often."

"Forgive this one that great weakness," M. de Grammont returned soothingly. "When he heard that one of the Bishop Bourne's assailants had been despatched by a Monsieur de Champvallon, and I assured him you would ask nothing of him for the service, he was so greatly pleased with you that he told me he would not be content until I brought you to entertain him and the ladies at Whitehall. So this very afternoon—"

"Ah, but no!"

"Ah, but yes!"

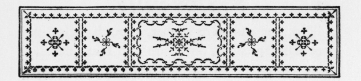

CHAPTER XVII

NEVER!" M. de Champvallon protested that kings should no longer be permitted to interfere with people; that the ideal government was a republic; that the mere sight of ladies would increase his melancholy, since for him henceforth all of them would be only painful mementoes of that brightest of them whom he had lost; and that far from being able to offer them any entertainment, all he wished to say to even the most beautiful was that he hoped to enter the monastery of M. La Trappe. Nevertheless, when he returned toward evening to the apartments he occupied at M. de Grammont's, he could not conceal from himself that he had

cut a figure at Whitehall somewhat gratifying.
Hints of his romantic story and of the poetic
quality of his grief had no doubt gone forth from
M. de Grammont judiciously; M. de Champvallon found himself regarded by the ladies with the
sympathetic and wistful glances they bestow
upon heroes whose sorrow they respect and hope
in proper time to alleviate. But his bereavement
was all too fresh, and to let his mind dwell upon
such triumphs would be unbecoming; in his
charming salon at M. de Grammont's he drooped
into a chair, sat in a gloomy posture and sighed
determinedly.

A valet brought him a letter. M. de Champvallon looked at it in the man's hand, whispered
"Already!" and almost followed an impulse to
wave the missive away without opening it. However, he took it and frowned as he saw that it
was sealed, apparently, with tar; then he looked
at the writing, smothered an outcry, sat straight,
trembling, opened the letter and read it.

"Most sweet deare frend Shanvalon this is writ
from the ship Hopeful the most pretty sweet
barque ever I saw and hath the stoutest pretty

seamen to man her all of such nimble grace when
they fly to the tops and the sails of such a white-
ness and swelling so richly in breezes with sea
birds calling their pretty notes and such a merry
world of blue and white all round about I doe
marvell how I lived all my life away from ships.
What I write will come to you by the sure hand
of our Lecky for hee stayed on shore and wee
have sailed to a harbour I need not name three
days from where wee first come onto the ship
and heere wee waited while Lecky looked privily
to some business for us and came hither with
much news. Soe hee will beare letters to reach
frends ashore when wee are upon the waters our
sailing for our Plantations in the provinces being
now sett for this very hour. By Lecky who is of
a pretty skill for inquiring privily in certaine
matters wee doe know what noble hand you had
and how lofty your behaviour for our coming
off in safety when there was soe hard a pinch
and soe wee are vaine to believe you would not
bee loath to have this knowledge of us. Wee could
have been wedded in the Frends fashion on board
the ship for wee had with us two of that faith
and I would gladly bee but my sweet love and

husband cannot bring himself to think hee is
though soe near it and wee did wait and come on
shore at this harbour where wee were wedded by
a prieste on the most pretty bright day of sun-
shine ever I saw and the seamen all in the bravest
cloathes and bob wiggs singing the most merry
songs when wee came again to the pretty ship.

"Now I will tell you that the little man you
saw that my husband preserved Francis Tanner
is of such a bright eloquence in religion I could
listen by the hour for hee doe truly glow with it
and hee tells mee there are Frends in your owne
country of France and I think when you shall
again bee there it would bee sweet to you to hear
what they say. But I cannot tell you that I am
yett of that faith for my faith is reposed with
all of mee in the hands of my sweet deare husband and I wait until wee bee decided by his
wisdom. Francis is of great hope that the light
will come to us ere wee reach our Plantations
and hee is a joyful frend to bee with us on this
brave ship where all are of a good spirit and
among the seamen much laughing and singing
but wee cannot love his wife soe well as him

though a prudent woman and not shrewish and more seemly than I first thought her. Yett I cannot think her soul is of soe high a gift as his and of the two hee is much the better companion as I have often marked and found my deare husband in agreement.

"Now my sweet deare frend Shanvalon I take leave of you in loveing farewell and with my sweet deare husband send such great thankes to you for the kindnesse towards us which you shewed that all wee could write to you in all our lives could not expresse our thankfulnesse and our loveingkindnesse to you. Soe now the seamen are shouting and singing nobly and wee sail forth and shall bee far on this pretty sea when you read and I desire you will find in your heart one little sweet thought to her your frend who prays God have you ever in the kindnesse of His hand and will ever bee like her deare husband,

"Your devoted faithful intirely loveing joyous servant   "J. Colpoys."

M. de Grammont, coming in an hour later, found the Chevalier freshly dressed in fine black silk, diamonds, raised point-lace of Venice, and wearing new black velvet shoes with silver heels and glitteringly buckled. From him, too, when his movements lightly stirred the air about him, there emanated hints of a rose perfume, delicately suggestive and never so acute as to detract from dignity. M. de Grammont, incomparably expert, bestowed the precious approval of a colleague.

"Perfection, no less! The full mode employed to express a condition of the heart! We are sad, yes—ah, we have our tender memories to mourn, yes!—but, on the other hand, we begin to forget a little, and, if the ladies make much of us, we do not insist that they shall pine forever! Perfection!"

M. de Champvallon did not deny that he might inspire this interpretation; but he had something to add to it. He gave his friend the letter to read; then said, "You speak of the condition of my heart; let me tell you it is both more sore and more happy—and also astonished by a discovery."

M. de Grammont looked up from the letter. "Good! Your heart has discovered—"

"For a time there did exist that wild bright picture
called Jeeny Feelmotte."

Looked out over the dark mass of London at night.

"No," M. de Champvallon said, becoming a precisionist. "It is my mind that makes the discovery. You said you would show me the wild new woman produced by this age, and for a time I believed you had done it. No, my friend, no! There is no such creature; it is only an appearance. It is a different manner in courtship—only a different manner and not a reality at all. Your new woman is a woman in every respect the same creature that always she was, which is but too plain as soon as the courting is happily finished. There never can be a new woman."

"No," M. de Grammont said reflectively, as he placed the letter upon a table. "You think not? But Meestress Jeeny Feelmotte—"

"Who?" the Chevalier said sadly and gravely. "She does not exist. There is a certain Madame Colpoys. This Madame Colpoys is precisely a young wife absorbed in the state of being her husband's wife, no more and no less to the end of her life. What was a poetic brightness, an appearance of fire sweeping across my sky, has been translated into a hearth-glow in the house of Colpoys. That is the loss for which my heart is the more sore, and now you will ask me what I have gained that makes it the more happy. Well, you will think me mystical; but for a time there did exist that wild bright picture painted in flame and called Jeeny Feelmotte, and it was I alone who saw it and knew it and understood all the strange beauty it possessed. This picture, then, I can keep forever. With a Madame Colpoys so perfectly a slave to her wifehood and so like ten thousand other young wives, I could never have anything to do."

This was his requiem for the married Jinny; yet it could not have been a complete expression of his thought of her. There must have been something more; for, even as he spoke, he turned to a window that showed the west, and, with his face unseen by his friend, looked out over the dark mass of London at night—looked indeed over it and beyond it to where a most pretty sweet barque sailed a sea that still at this hour was sunlit.

M. de Grammont, waiting sympathetically for some moments, was of the opinion that Jinny had her desire.

34858